# THE JACKET TRICK

# THE JACKET TRICK

## ANDRÉ HANSSON

André Hansson
2014

First Printing: 2014

ISBN 978-1-291-81806-2

André Hansson
www.andrehansson.com

*For Dorota*

# 1

"INCOMING!" Hugo yelled as he dove head first into Bernie's cubicle. Bernie had one of the larger ones so there he could hide. He dove in and rolled on the floor like he was ducking a grenade. He banged his knee hard against the metal leg of Bernie's desk. It stung like hell. He hit the nerve, of course, sending an electric jolt up his leg to his groin. He let out a shriek but quickly put a hand over his mouth to kill it.

"What the fuck, Hugs...?" Bernie said.

"Shhh! The Playboy boss is on my ass. He wants to meet and discuss what it is I do here."

"So you wanna be quiet and not reveal your position, is that it?"

"Yeah."

"Makes sense. Except for part where you yelled 'incoming!' at the top of your lungs."

Hugo smiled as best he could. The pain still radiated throughout the leg. It was in his balls now too. Maybe he accidently squeezed one when he rolled around.

"It's a style thing," he said, grinning as the pain crept

towards his tonsils.

*Yep. Definitely squeezed a ball.*

"You know," he continued. "It just had to be done. Come what may."

Bernie the *old-timer* looked more rugged today than he usually did. People called him *the old-timer* because he was the oldest employee at FastCredit, despite being only fifty-one. Like Hugo, he was an American, trapped here in London's financial sector. His job was to maintain the bank's various databases and provide hard numbers for the analysts. But just like Hugo, in these days of perpetual financial crisis, he probably didn't do much real work anymore.

Right now he was sitting in front of his screen, smiling so widely he was showing gum above those slightly coffee-stained teeth. When someone smiles or laughs in front of a screen in an office it's a dead giveaway that they're doing something other than working. He was probably amusing himself with that clip of a man getting his head stuck in an elephant's ass that had been passed around in a traditionally NSFW-marked email this morning.

*Weird.*

Bernie was the very one who had taught Hugo to laugh on the inside so it wouldn't show. He guessed Bernie didn't care if he was caught not working.

Bernie looked up from the screen and pointed towards the hallway.

"Speaking of... here he comes, Hugs."

Yep. There he was. The Playboy boss. He was the top dog here.

*The big man. The numero uno honcho. The head cheese!*

8

He wasn't Hugo's boss directly. His boss had quit yesterday and that's why the Playboy boss wanted to speak to him. Find out what he did here. Hugo didn't feel up for that talk today. So, hiding was the only thing he could come up with.

The Playboy boss's real name was Bryce. Hugo called him the Playboy boss because he looked like a Ken doll at the Playboy Mansion. Early forties, bleached hair, fake tan. He also wore some sort of lip gloss. It was discreet, but still obvious if you just gave it an extra look. He was, like everyone else in the top senior management of a bank, into golf. He practiced his swing in the hallway outside his office. Sometimes in his office, but then without the club. The ceiling was too low there.

He was approaching. Hugo dragged himself and his temporarily bum leg towards the corner of the cubicle. He pressed up gently against the inside of the wall, pulling his legs towards him in a sitting fetus position. He would be safe as long the bastard didn't enter the cubicle.

Hugo exchanged a glance with Bernie. He would cover for him. He always did. Bernie cared as little about this job as anyone and wouldn't care if he got caught in a lie. Even in one as ridiculous as this one.

"Have you seen Hugo?" the Playboy boss said.

Bernie shook his head. "No."

"Where is he? I've been looking for him all day."

"I was just with him," Bernie lied. "At his desk. Did you check there?"

The Playboy boss sighed. "I was just there!"

"Maybe he's just getting coffee or something?"

Then the Playboy Boss stepped inside the cubicle, just past the opening. He started talking shop. Data warehouse stuff, shit that Bernie worked with.

*Fuck!*

The last thing Hugo wanted was idle conversation. All the Playboy boss had to do was look to his right and he would be busted. Bernie was completely unfazed. Didn't even flinch and look in his direction, which certainly would've made the Playboy boss look too. The conversation droned on. Hugo's leg hurt. His balls hurt. He was suddenly aware of the fact that he was feeling queasy.

*Must be from the ball pain.*

Bernie did his best to end the conversation but people in the banking business love to chat about their boring jobs. Especially people at the Playboy boss's level. Whenever they said anything they had to follow it up with bits and pieces of conversation which would cover their asses if they happened to talk about anything that could be construed as a statement of fact, opinion, or decision. Avoiding accountability for anything and everything—that was the main purpose of any words that came out their mouths.

The conversation droned on. Hugo zoned out. He didn't catch anything of what they were talking about. He just registered the tone of voice. And when that tone signaled the conversation was coming to an end, he snapped back in. The Playboy boss would be turning to leave. The only question was if he would turn to his left or right. Left was fine. Right was not.

"Okay," said the Playboy boss. "If you see Hugo, let me know."

He turned. To his right.

"I will!" Bernie said. Loudly. It sounded unnatural, which of course was the plan. It worked. The Playboy boss turned back. Bernie got up and walked him out instead, making him turn to his left as they both left. Brilliant, as the Brits would say. Bernie had the kind of smoothness with cheating that only years of experience would get you.

Hugo listened as the voices faded away. He got up from the floor and sat down in the extra chair and waited for Bernie to come back. He took a couple of deep breaths to force himself to calm down.

Bernie's part of the office was livelier than his. His cubicle was adjacent to the front office, which was always busy. Young Generation Y:ed boys and girls born in the Eighties populated this part of the business, constantly milling about between phone calls, printers, archives and their computers. FastCredit was the type of bank that only provided customer services by phone so there were only clients in the office on exceptional basis. The back office staff, which both Bernie and Hugo were part of, was a little bit older, if only slightly. FastCredit was a young business.

Hugo noticed the new art on the walls, rented of course. They were switched out every other week or so. Financial crises never affect this kind of fine polish that all banks love so much.

Bernie came back, now with a bunch of paper in his hands. Rule number one in a bank, or any office job for that matter, is to always carry papers in your hand when you are away from your desk. If you don't people will immediately assume that you're not working. Emails

11

are fine. Bernie printed every single one as soon as he got them. They look official and *work-related*. These particular emails weren't his, of course, since he didn't have them in his hand when he walked Bryce out.

"Grabbed it from the printer," he said and threw them in the trash as he sat down behind the desk. Whoever those papers really belonged to would simply have to print new ones.

"So, what's up, kid?" Bernie said. His voice was coarse. Hugo hadn't noticed before with all the commotion.

"Out trolling for booty last night?" he asked.

"Naw. Just wing-manned a buddy of mine. Took a hit for him so that he could get his hands on the pretty one. Hence the extra booze. Hence the hangover."

"Say no more." Actually, he wasn't completely sure what that meant. Hugo had never been that good at picking up girls.

Bernie had the reputation for being something of a pick-up artist despite not being all that attractive. A PUA, as he abbreviated it. He wasn't ugly or anything, just rugged and kinda worn out from hard living. Like an older James Franco. These days he wasn't that active. He was more like a grand master passing on his knowledge to the younger generation. He had offered to take Hugo under his wing more than once.

"With women it's all about *personality*," he always said. "What you say, your body language, eye contact, confidence. The right kind of *behavior* will trigger a woman's attraction buttons. Good looks will help you, of course, but it's not a deciding factor."

He never bragged about his conquests. *A gentleman*

*doesn't do that,* he always said. An alpha male doesn't need others to validate him. He's comfortable in himself.

Usually Bernie wasn't this hungover. The girls must've put up quite a fight last night. Hugo could smell the booze from five feet away. Bernie's very distinctive hangover smell usually comprised of a mix of peppermint from his gums, mixed with coffee and just a hint of a pick-me-up. Today the emphasis was clearly on the pick-me-up. He fished the old pocket flask out of the bottom drawer. He looked around to make sure no one saw, then he took a sip and immediately after folded a new Juicy Fruit into his cheek. He offered the flask to Hugo who always politely turned the offer down.

"Mind if I stay here for a while?" Hugo said. "If Bryce shows up again we're discussing some pressing work issues. Okay?"

"Sure, kid." Bernie scratched his three day stubble and then took another sip. He put the flask back in the drawer.

"So," Bernie said. "What about the new boss?"

"Starts in two weeks. No more freedom."

His old boss had been the hands-off kind. She had let Hugo do whatever he wanted as long as he had delivered what he was supposed to. That sort of freedom was rare in this business. Hugo knew the chances of getting that again with a new boss, whoever it may be, were slim to none.

"Maybe it won't be that bad," Bernie said, as if he had read his mind. Hugo just smiled.

"Naw, you're right," Bernie said. "It will be that bad."

13

"I don't know, I just feel so demotivated lately. And a new boss won't help. Thinking about trying to revive my writing. Again."

"Yes, you've mentioned that a few times the last few weeks. Stop talking about it and just do it."

"I thought I was at peace with leaving it behind, but apparently I'm not. But it's not that easy to get anything done when you have work sixty hours a week. Which is what I will need to put in with the new boss. And during weekends I have to play house with Jess. She'd kill me if I'd spend our couple's together time writing."

"So quit!"

"Can't. Mortgage, student loans. Expensive lifestyle. The money prison, dude. You know, the more you make, the more you lock yourself in."

"Sounds like a bunch of excuses to me."

They were excuses. They were also real problems. How had other people who had succeeded in writing done it before him? Did they sponge off their respective others? Doesn't sound like the right thing to do. Did they live in a box on the street, with an old typewriter, writing on the back of old sandwich wrappers? He and Jess couldn't manage anymore without two relatively high incomes. Not without serious downsizing. Jess had never liked his writing interest. *A childish boyhood dream,* she called it. She'd never put up with living in a flat share out in Hounslow somewhere, eating beans and canned tuna for dinner every day, waiting for the bathroom while the weird roommate jerks off holding a pair of her dirty panties to his nose. All while he was waiting for his big break as a writer.

He could potentially put in an hour's work in the

14

evening when he got home, when Jess was at the gym but he was just too tired. And he had to go to the gym himself. The body doesn't stay slim all by itself after thirty.

*Oh well. I'll retire someday.*

"Let's go get coffee," Bernie said.

They stopped by Nella's desk first. She wasn't there so they waited. Unlike Hugo and Bernie, Nella was still ambitious about her job. She was still partially in the management's corner and rarely agreed with the criticisms Hugo and Bernie slammed them with (behind their backs, of course). She was part of their gang anyway. Besides, Hugo and Nella went way back, to their college days when they had met in Economics 101. Mornings were not her strong suit and it was best to stay clear before ten. She joined the living after a few cups of coffee.

After a few minutes she swaggered in with her slightly tomboyish walk, hair up as always, with a smile on her lips. She wore make-up but it was very discreet, so discreet that you didn't notice it at all unless you had seen her without it for comparison. Hugo had, so he knew. The smiled revealed that she had had her coffee.

"More coffee?" she said.

They both nodded. Her full name was Petronella but everyone just shortened it to Nella and had done so since she was a little girl. Only customs officials and other government authority figures ever said her real name. Hugo sometimes called her Nells, or even Nellsy. It was only fair. After all, she was the one who had come up with his nickname, Hugs.

"I only have a few minutes before I have another

15

meeting, so we can't go downstairs," she said.

*Downstairs* meant the lobby down by the main reception. There was a small corner with a sofa group and a better coffee machine. It was slightly secluded and almost always empty, and could therefore be used to safely unload about your idiot boss, or anyone else that annoyed you for that matter.

Instead they went to pantry number two in the back office section. They each got themselves an acid-loaded cup of coffee and sat down in the IKEA sofa.

Nella had the most dangerous job in the entire bank. She transferred money between the front end computer system and the back end computer system. These two very costly systems didn't communicate with each other so it all had to be done manually using a simple spreadsheet. Non-communicating patchworks of systems is a disturbingly common occurrence in banks. If people only knew.

The risk of screwing up those transfers was enormous. A simple typo, a zero too many or too few would result in a total clusterfuck. Management, of course, preferred living with this risk over investing in a proper solution. It was all so stupid it was almost beautiful. If you did screw up it would mean that management could think they had more money to play with than they actually did. They would then spend it and then it would all be fucked. But Nella wasn't scared. She faced the stupidity head on. And so far no incidents.

"So, what do you think about this afternoon?" Bernie said. He almost whispered. In the pantries up in the office you had to watch what you said. There were many ears, and office people love to gossip.

"I don't know," said Nella.

"Maybe it's time?" Hugo said.

Nelly was immediately annoyed. "Let's not take anything out in advance. You don't know it's about cutbacks."

Hugo smiled but didn't say anything. He didn't have to.

On the way back to his desk he took the short cut through Management's corridor. Bryce was in his office, practicing his swing. Hugo scurried past undetected.

*By all means. The business is going down the shithole. Why should he work?*

The meeting turned out to be just another piece of corporate team-building bullshit. Strategies and goals and whatnot. Hugo slept through most of it. No cutbacks announced this time. But they would come eventually.

**2**

Friday afternoon. Reporting week. Hugo had submitted everything and was done for the day. The week had eaten away at him with ten hour workdays every day except Monday, but he had made it. Now his reward was waiting for him with the weekend and dinner with friends. He should have felt content, proud, maybe even happy? But there was something missing.

He packed up his laptop and a few reports that were going to require some attention over the weekend. That used to be okay for a while. The first year after he had started here. But now he mentally threw up on anything relating to work, especially if it was outside office hours.

He waved goodbye to Bernie and headed for the front door. The front office had been empty for two, three hours now when everyone had rushed to pick up kids at school or to get a bottle of wine for tonight's dinner.

Hugo didn't know why exactly he felt like he did. Sure, the work was crap but he had liked it at least a little in the past. Tolerated it, was perhaps a more appropriate word. It definitely wasn't the pay. Of that he was sure. In the past he had been able to drop things once he was out of the office but now it was spilling over into his private time. Everything seemed kind of...*deflated*. Like a flat beer. Sure, it goes down but the taste... He wasn't angry. He wasn't depressed. But he wasn't the opposite either.

*Lethargic?*

*Apathetic?*

Isn't that the same thing? What was the word he was looking for? Maybe he was just tired?

On the subway home he took out one of his old short stories he had written in college. He had planned on editing it for a long time now. Maybe bang it into publishable shape so that the story he had miraculously sold to Science Fiction and Fantasy five years ago could have its follow-up.

He read the text. Was it good? Was it not? He couldn't tell. A few years ago he would've known exactly what was wrong, exactly what was right and then made the necessary changes. Now he had stared at the same line every day for three weeks and come up with nothing.

*Nothing.*

Maybe he was just tired? Or maybe he just was an untalented hack? Writers, the good ones, always had an interesting history to pull from. An abusive childhood. Maybe they had done time. Killed someone, whatever. Hugo's demon was that he had no demons. He had had a nice, safe suburban childhood. No crime. No abuse. No painful losses of loved ones. Nothing to draw on. No wonder he had constant writer's block.

He told himself he'd give the story another try sometime during the weekend, but he knew he wouldn't feel like it then. On weekends his brain wanted to shut down. He wanted to go downtown. Shop a little and have some lunch with Jess. Things that didn't require any intellectual effort. He wanted that. He *needed* it so that he could recharge.

Tonight the reward would consist of a dinner at Will and Sarah's place. Hugo and Jessica were to bring the wine so he stopped at Tesco. There was a line. Everybody wants booze and snacks for Friday night. He picked up two bottles of Cabernet-Sauvignonsomething. Some French stuff. Nice. Since he got the job at FastCredit they could afford more expensive wines

*At least something is moving in the right direction.*

He remembered how excited he had been the day he got the call back from FastCredit. Now he was going to make a lot of money. Work long hours, but that was okay. He had taken on everything thrown his way with the greatest enthusiasm. The first year he had even had energy left over to write in the evenings. He was still ambitious at work. Enjoyed it, really. Jess had even been fine with him spending a few hours after work writing. The protests that it ate up all their couple time came later.

Jessica was in the kitchen when he got in the door. She had prepared a whiskey sour for him and put out some light snacks before dinner.

"Hey, baby," he said and gave her a kiss on the cheek. He took the drink and smiled. "You read my mind."

"A lot at work?"

He nodded.

"We have to leave right away."

*That's right!*

He had already forgotten that he'd come home almost three hours later than normal. It was almost eight already.

"Can't we be fashionably late? I just have to kick back a little first."

He sank down on the couch and threw his feet on the table. He tossed his tie on the floor and unbuttoned another button on his shirt.

*Maybe this very moment on Friday nights is the entire reward for working?*

Jessica gave him an annoyed look. He knew she didn't like it when he had his feet on the table (which was some expensive Danish designer thing she had picked). But she didn't say anything. Maybe she just wanted him to get a move on.

She was already dressed. Black party dress cut just above the knee and high heels. Maybe just a little too much make-up but he'd take it in a heartbeat. Hair up. Maybe new highlights. Jessica was a brunette but he had never seen her in anything else than a light blonde except in old photos from before they met. Tonight she looked stunning.

*Maybe stay home and do something else...?*

"I have to take a shower," he said. "Put some other clothes on."

"But get moving then!"

British accents are cute but can be so annoying when they take on that whining tone. He moaned as he got up from the couch. A bit higher than necessary. It wasn't just the going out part, but also to whom. Hugo hated Will and Sarah. They were Jessica's friends originally and he had never really gotten along with them. There were no open conflicts or any such thing, of course. He just thought they were so unbelievably boring.

He chugged down the rest of the whiskey and went to the bathroom.

"Just a quick shower," he said again. "Three minutes. Tops. Got to wash away all the office dust."

*Okay. I don't hate Will and Sarah. Right?*

There was nothing wrong with them, really. They were good people. They had similar jobs to him and Jessica. They were business majors, just like they were. Didn't like the same kind of movies but you can hardly hate someone for that, can you? Anyway, Hugo never wanted to go and yawned reflexively inside himself whenever Jess told him they had been invited over to them, or when she had invited them.

Maybe it was the entire concept he hated? *Couples Hell!* Apparently, it was a phase in life everyone had to pass through, except that once entered, the phase never seemed to reach its end. It was cyclical. It was like an eternal purgatory where Paradise always remained an arm's length away. Bad analogy. There probably isn't any paradise.

Couples Hell is the last gasping breaths of your youth. It starts with childhood. Everyone complains about their childhood but Hugo really couldn't say he had a bad one. As an adult it is comforting to have a bad childhood on which you can blame everything that goes wrong in your life. Even a dead writing career.

As a child he had to put up with a few nicknames.

Hugo became Hugh, which became Hugh Hefner. Hugo didn't know who that was until much later but he still didn't like it. Sometimes it became Huey which became Chopper. He did have wild hair which conceivably could have been the rotors of a chopper, but it was farfetched. He thought so already then, but sometimes the imagination of children is as endless as their cruelty.

After childhood come the awkward teen years with all their rebellious antics and debuts of various kinds. Sex. Alcohol. Weed. The intensity of those memories had started to fade away. Today they belonged to a different reality. He sometimes wondered if other thirty-plus people felt the same way.

The twenties is all about rambunctious single life. Nightclubs. Lots of booze and weed every weekend. In those days he had had a remarkable resistance to hangovers. Where was that today?

At thirty your friends start to pair up and after a few years you have no social contacts whatsoever that do not include couples. Quiet evenings, dinners with two or three pairs, with wine, coffee and liquor on the side.

*Liquor!*

Is it a sign of maturity when you take your coffee with *liquor* on the side? Or even worse, is a sign of maturity when you realize you actually *like it!* Every Friday evening the ritual begins again. Sometimes even on Saturdays. After a few years all possible conversation topics have been run through so many times you start to contemplate suicide. But at the same time you don't want to go back to any of the previous iterations of the cycle. They're history. You long for something else but you just don't know what. It is exactly this lost longing that defines Couples Hell.

After the shower he went to the liquor cabinet to pour himself a new drink. Bernie called it a *perseverance drink*. Alcohol consumed for purpose of making something unpleasant go down easier.

*Social lubrication. Keep it greasy so it'll go down easy.*

Hugo needed one of those now.

*What's the difference between a drink and a cocktail?*

One of life's really big issues. He, Nella and Bernie had discussed it animatedly at the last company thing. After drinking several of them, of course.

"Cocktails are not something hip young people drink," Nella had said.

"A cocktail has more than two ingredients," Hugo had said. "A drink only two. Booze and soda."

"No, no, no. It's..."

Blah, blah, blah. Drunken gibberish...

Finally Bernie, who had been quiet up to this point, had banged his fist on the table so hard he knocked over his scotch and said:

"If there's a fucking umbrella in it, it's a cocktail."

And then that was that.

He dressed. A suit and a white shirt, no tie. Dressed down in Hugo's world. He would remove his jacket once he arrived and that would be as casual as he ever got when seeing other people.

"The cab is here," Jessica said from the kitchen. "Hurry up, Hugo!"

Jess never called him Hugs.

He downed the drink in one sweep (and it was a drink since there was no umbrella) and put on his shoes and overcoat. He was just the right amount of tipsy now. He would manage until the conversation wine was served.

They didn't say much in the taxi. Hugo felt how a week's hard work began to take its toll. He wasn't sure Jess felt the same. She didn't have the kind of periodic pressure he had, even though they had similar jobs. For her the burden was spread evenly, something he sometimes envied. But she didn't have those nice stretches of calm that he had. He appreciated the exhaustion from the peaks. The silence that followed in their wake was refreshing.

A year ago Will and Sarah had taken another step in the cycle. They had had a kid. Hugo found it both strange and disturbing that whenever someone has a kid their own identity takes off into nowhere. Only the kid exists. You know that for years to come that every Christmas card you'll get will have a picture of the kid only, even if the greetings are from the entire family. Every profile pic on Facebook will be exchanged for a picture of the child and you'll know that you won't be able to have a conversation with any of the parents about anything except matters related to child-rearing without them suddenly losing interest. No more beer nights. No sports talk. No movies talk. No nothing.

Hugo and Jessica had congratulated the lucky parents with a card that said "Congrats to the boy. See you in twenty years!" Jessica had only reluctantly agreed to buying it. Hugo had found it in the novelty section but he failed to see the humor in it. He was still baffled by how Will, who had dove head on into the role of being a dad, had just let go of everything he was before. Now he could just interrupt a conversation, mid-sentence, to attend to some need the child had. And it wasn't just when the kid had fallen and hit his head or the like. But for *any little thing*. The thought that one's identity could just sink in and wither away like that amazed him. It scared him.

*I'm such cliché sometimes.*

Hugo liked kids. At least that's what he told himself. He thought they were cute and all, like puppies, but the thought of having his own frightened him. Jessica, on the other hand, was absolutely delighted. She was fluent in cuddly baby talk. Better than the kid's parents.

They all stuck rigidly to the script for the entire dinner. A sweet aperitif was served (and this was definitely a cocktail since it had an umbrella in it). Sarah said it was a Cosmopolitan. For the appetizer they had asparagus soup. The entrée consisted of a chocolate-marinated tenderloin. Everything was amazing, of course. Cooking was all the rage now with all those damned kitchen TV shows. Will and Sara had jumped on the bandwagon accordingly. For dessert they had a panna cotta and then coffee. And *liquor*.

Will and Sarah were dog people. Or used to be. Before they had the kid they (and Jess) had cuddled with the dog the same way they now cuddled with the baby. These days the dog was always locked out on the balcony when Hugo and Jessica were visiting. Ostracized. Made redundant. Out in the cold, literally since it was January and freezing outside. Hugo had thought many times about saying something but never did.

The dinner conversation revealed that another step in the cycle was about to be conquered. The move to the suburbs. When a couple buys a house, all the time that is not spent on the kids will be spent on the house. You could tell already. Amortizations, interest rates, new kitchen, interior design issues all dominated the conversation solidly. Hugo was quiet most of the time but Jessica was enthusiastically engaged.

Hugo had found Will obnoxious already way before the last steps of the cycle had been conquered. He had been the type who cited famous scholars and thinkers in conversations as soon as the opportunity presented itself. And sometimes when it didn't. He inserted Latin and French into his sentences whenever he could. He would say things like *"Le Boulangerie* is *de facto vis a vis* the *Palais de Justice."* Or incomprehensible things like, "you can't assume *a priori* a *tabula rasa* within a *postmodernist ethos."*

*You wanna seem educated. We get it!*

All of this was now blown away when diapers and mortgages started to dominate. Hugo was pretty sure he liked the old Will better, even if both of them were decidedly tedious.

The rest of the evening ran by in sort of a haze. Hugo had consciously downed one or two extra glasses of wine to make everything go by easier. The three of them droned on for the entire evening about IKEA furniture, various living space measurements and station wagons. Hugo nodded whenever he suspected they wanted something from him. Late in the night they said good-bye and the obligatory "let's do this again soon" and then they were off.

In the cab Jess had that look. She was horny from all the talking about kids, family and suburban bliss. She always got that way after cuddling with babies. The idea of starting a family of her own was her trigger. In fact, these days it was her *only* trigger.

"Let's get one of those ourselves," she would say.

"Sure," Hugo would say, even though he didn't really mean it.

He had used this many times to get himself off. He'd cuddle with babies of friends and relatives, he'd speak baby talk with them, all in an effort to manipulate Jess into having sex later when they were alone. Tonight he hadn't done anything like that but she was still horny. Or *randy*, as she would say.

She was all over him. Kissing him, whispering naughty stuff into his ear.

"Maybe I'll give you a blowjob right here in the cab?"

"You wouldn't have the guts to do that."

"Really?"

Her hand went down to his pants. She unzipped him and grabbed his cock. He was getting a boner. She had a most delightful look in her eyes, he had to admit. One of both embarrassment and naughtiness. The cab driver probably saw it but it didn't matter. It was one of those funky English cabs with a lot of space in the back. She went down.

Hugo had to admit to himself that he was a little shocked. He had never thought Jess would ever do such a thing. It was nice but he wasn't really into it. It wasn't that it was public—he didn't care if the driver saw anything. It was the reason for Jess's excitement that bothered him. Before he wouldn't have minded that it wasn't really him that made her horny, but tonight it annoyed him. It couldn't go on this way forever. Sooner or later he would have to deal with the fact that it

28

wasn't Hugo himself that got her going, but some evolutionary-instilled imperative to procreate.

*Isn't it always like that? It is, isn't it?* So why should he care? She's horny, so just man up and hit dat ass! It still bothered him, though. It still wasn't him. It was the image of a nursery with pink elephants and rainbows on the walls, a cradle, a luxury kitchen, of a picket fence, of IKEA furniture that got her going. It was like she could do it with anyone, as long as this dream was the end result.

She didn't have time to finish before they were home. Hugo zipped himself up while Jess paid the driver.

"Good evening," the driver simply said like nothing had happened.

In the bedroom they continued. She ripped his clothes off and pushed him down onto the bed. She straddled him and rode herself to a furious orgasm. It didn't take long at all. Hugo thought he'd finish himself off quickly with some regular mish but he couldn't come. He was too bothered by the cuddly baby crap.

She turned over and got on all fours. It usually helped. Everything became tighter doggy style. Heavier stimulation. But he still couldn't come.

"You want the ass," she said.

He thought about it. He was bothered but still worked up now and wanted to unload. He had always found anal to be a little overrated. Fun the first few times, but then just tedious. It wasn't like in the pornos. In real life you can get dookie all over your dick.

He remembered a friend telling him how he had fucked this girl in the ass, doggy style. He was drunk and a bit nauseous to begin with and when he came and pulled out, a glorious mixture of cum, blood and shit had oozed out of the girl's asshole and he had shit all over his dick. He had been so disgusted he threw up all over her back.

Fecal matter aside, you can't just do it like Rocco and spit on it and shove it in. At least not with Jess. It would require an exorbitant amount of lube and twenty minutes of easing it in gently. He didn't think he was up for it tonight.

"Let's just call it," he said. "I probably drank too much wine." A good lie, wine did make him sleepy and gave him a blocked nose. Sometimes his performance would be affected. Credible, but still a lie.

Jess wouldn't give up. She took him in the mouth again and kept at it until he started feeling raw but nothing happened. It was good but he just couldn't get over that final hump and shoot his load. Eventually she gave up.

"It's okay," he said. "It's not you."

*Why is it so hard to be honest with the person you're sharing your life with?*

In a way it wasn't her. Visual cues were usually enough for Hugo to get turned on and Jess was grade A fuck meat. A real trophy. Very beautiful, doll-like facial features, perfectly delicate and symmetrical. Flat belly and round hips. Not model skinny, but still not an ounce of excess fat. Her breasts were crazy beautiful, smallish the way Hugo liked them. Today it wasn't enough.

They lay on the bed and didn't talk for a while. To Jess this probably wasn't a big deal. Things like this happened from time to time, to both of them. But it was usually because trivial reasons like too much booze or physical fatigue.

*Ahh, fuck it.*

He had a tendency to over-analyze everything.

"You were so quiet tonight," Jessica said.

"I was just tired."

"Were you bored?"

"No. I was just tired."

He sensed that she wanted to talk more. She wanted to dig into it, his insistent silence during the evening, turn it inside out, turn it into something big. She always wanted to do that, but she didn't say anything else. He was grateful. He just wanted to sleep it off. They held each other while they drifted off.


The week started off easy. It always did after the monthly reporting is done. Monday went by, Tuesday went by. Not much to do. It was as if the entire business had a hangover and needed to chill a bit from vomiting all those work hours the week before. Hugo spent most of his time surfing the net. Benzo's and Bernie's various YouTube clips and some other junk also kept him busy.

He thought more and more about how boring his job really was. He worked with what the banking world calls risk management, a prestigious analytics job requiring years of training, without really being all that complicated. It is a job that impresses people. Hugo worked with *mathematical models*. Forecasts and whatnot. It always sounds good when you say you are working with *models*. It seems sophisticated, advanced and fun while at the same time being incomprehensible to lay-men. Incomprehensible must mean difficult and if you work with something difficult you must be good? But all it really meant was that you spent your days shuffling decimals around in spreadsheets.

Wednesday drifted by in the same pace as the two previous days. Maybe there was a slight tendency for the wheels to start rolling again. He spoke to a few front-office colleagues and they were quite busy. Not so strange, really. Departments who had customer contacts didn't have the same rollercoaster workload as Hugo's job had.

He studied the rental art on the walls. These were new (they were switched out every third or fourth week or so). There was some nudity this time, naturally surrealistically portrayed. A boob here, another one there. Crooked, off angle. Etcetera. This nudity had stirred up some indignant emotion in the management team and with some others. All water cooler jabber was about this for the entire past week.

*Apparently people in this place have missed that the net is full to the brim with porn. Just three clicks and you can watch some hairy guy sink his entire fist into the ass of tiny Asian girl while she has her mouth full of BBC at the other end.*

In a world like that, how can a fluffy little oil-painted boob be so upsetting? The perversities the net offered of course can't be enjoyed in a bank. The security filter saw to that.

Wednesdays was after work night. He, Nella and Nicolas met for beers at a place called *The Red Tick* in the City of London. It was a tradition dating back to the days when they all had just landed their first job after college. Nella and Hugo had eventually ended up here at FastCredit while Nicolas had stayed with Chase, where they had all went through their financial services boot camp.

When Hugo arrived Nella and Nicolas had already parked themselves in their regular booth in the back, in a corner by the bar. They sipped cautiously on their beers as if they didn't want to start their regular binge drinking before Hugo arrived. He was forty minutes late so he hoped they were still on their first one. It's always tough to be left behind.

Peter Lawrence was the proprietor of *The Red Tick*, and a fat bastard. He was better known as Lardence, or Lardy for short. Lardy didn't mind. He liked food. Especially deep fried food. He had no problem admitting he was a fat bastard. He had no plans to stop eating either. When someone brought up that he shouldn't tolerate people calling him fat he always just shrugged and said, "I am a fat bastard. I'd rather be a fat bastard than a model if it means I have to eat salads."

*Who wouldn't?*

Lardy finished up their little quartet. They had all spent so much time at *The Tick* he had almost become a friend. Lardence had a distinct small business owner background and had opened *The Tick* about the same time as the others had started their jobs. He had to manage the bar but mostly kept within conversational distance, ready to throw in some annoying comment in between taking customer orders.

*The Tick* was named after a beer that Moe the bartender had served Homer in an episode of The Simpsons when Homer had asked for something special besides Duff. Lardy, who possessed surprising artistic talent, had himself painted a portrait on the wall above the bar of Moe holding one of the Red Tick bottles saying, "Needs more dog!" Most of everything else was standard British pub. Dark wood, some carved inlays for decoration, chalk board menu, the works. Everything looked worn and old as hell but it was made to look that way. Fake. All of it. Nobody cared.

"The prodigal son," Lardy said as Hugo sat down. He already pulled a beer that he gently slid over the counter to Hugo's hand.

Lardy almost always wore t-shirts with prints on them. He wore a new one almost every time they met. This one said 'Enough about me, let's talk about *me*'.

"The boss-less son," Hugo said as he took his seat next to Nella.

"So what?" Nicolas said. "Shit like that happens all the time in this business."

"Yeah, poor you," Nella said.

They all mistook his comment for whining. Hugo liked having no boss.

Nicolas had also taken quite a few steps in the cycle of life. He had met his Anna fairly quickly after graduation and now had two kids. A boy and girl? Hugo didn't keep track that closely. But yeah, he was almost a hundred percent sure. Boy and a girl. Around two, three years old now.

Hugo wasn't sure if it was Nicolas's newish role as a father or something else, but he gave a much older impression these days. Like, really old. He guessed it was true what they said, you only fully become an adult when you have kids of your own.

It wasn't just that he felt older, he looked older. He was a victim of a typical thirty-plus syndrome. His hairline had receded somewhat and left a thin tousle at the top of his forehead which he still styled in a bedhead fashion. He picked at it constantly, as if to make sure it was still there. Hugo found the whole thing incredibly entertaining.

"So what are you going to do about it?" Nicolas said.

"With the boss, you mean?"

"Yeah. What else?"

"I guess there's nothing I can do."

"Why all the whining then? I know you. You have something on your mind." There! He picked at his bedhead tousle again, restyling it a bit, so it would point straight up.

When Nella finally arrived she had Benzo with her. He was welcome, of course.

"I'm so fucking sick of office work," Hugo said when everyone was seated (they never stood outside). "It blows even under the best of circumstances. I mean, consider what we do for a second. We shuffle paper, then we shuffle more paper and then we shuffle some more paper again! I'm sure Hell is a place where everyone is forced to do office work twenty-four-seven. Put papers in binder, take them out of binders, move them from one binder to another, sign them, attest them, edit them, void them, copy, revise, file, destroy, collate until your fingertips bleed ink.

"And that's not all. We also have the paper-shuffling's computerized cousin, moving decimals around in a spreadsheet. Everything to the beat of some

35

toxic boss's drum."

Hugo took a sip from his beer. A big one. He looked at Nella, who gave him the ol' stink eye. She didn't like it when he picked on the banking industry. Like she took it personally, or something. He didn't care.

"This has been my life the last five years," he continued. "Up early, Corn Flakes and coffee for breakfast every goddamned morning, the Tube to work, shuffle papers, surf the net, shuffle some more papers, more surf, move around decimals, surf even more, put papers in a binder, move decimals, surf yet again, the Tube home, work out so you don't sack up, watch a little TV with Jess, possibly some routine sex if I'm very, very lucky, then finally sleep. And then as soon as your head hits the pillow the alarm goes off and it starts all over again. Up early, Corn Flakes, Tube, shuffle papers, et-fucking-cetera.

"Every fucking day is the same. I just don't know if I can do this for another *four decades* before I finally get to retire. Life's not short, it's *too long*!"

He took a sip to wet his throat. He was getting sore. "I'm letting the days go by, I'm letting the water hold me down. Then after a lifetime of paper shuffling I'll be old and arthritic. A crumpled-up geezer dreaming about the good ol' days. Too worn out to do anything, let alone revive those youthful ideals and dreams that I'm at this very point in my life unmercifully drowning. What's the point?"

Nicolas smiled, one of those sarcastic smiles people give you when they don't take what you say seriously. "Welcome to adulthood. That's what life looks like for all of us. Just join the rat race and try to look happy. I

36

mean, I also have dreams about doing something more exciting but you have to work, don't you?"

"I just want my life to have some sort meaningful purpose," Hugo continued, unabated by Nicolas's protest. "Something measurable, something that proved I was ever here. A contractor can point to a house he built and say 'I made that', the writer can say 'I wrote that book'. What can someone working in a bank say? 'I shuffled those papers'? No, you can't even say that because after five years they're moved to some storage in Alaska or who knows where and after another five they're destroyed. What's left after that? What have you left behind that you can say 'I did that' about? It's like you never even existed."

He paused and took a sip. "I need to be *reborn*! Reborn into something else. And if anyone of you say 'why don't you work in an advertising agency, they're creative' I swear I will smack you. That's not what I mean by being reborn!"

They all laughed. Possibly a pity laugh, not a ha-ha funny laugh. It was hard to say. He gave them the finger for good measure.

"Working in a bank isn't that bad," Nella said. "It's what I *want* to do."

"*Want* to do? Nobody *wants* to work in a bank, Nella. It's just something you do when your real dreams didn't come true. Ask a thousand kids what they want to do when they grow up. Not one of them is gonna say 'work in a bank'."

"Way to shit all over my career choice."

She looked angry now but he couldn't stop himself. Couldn't or wouldn't? It didn't matter. On he went.

"Saying it's a choice is just a rationalization to convince yourself your life isn't crappy. It's a compromise, a lie you tell yourself so you don't have to face the fact that your life didn't turn out the way you wanted it to. But one day it's going to hit you. And you'll want a do-over. Well, guess what? You can't have one 'cause now you're old and your ball sack is hanging down between your knees. Fuck, fuck, fuckity, fuck-fuck-fuck!"

Now she looked really angry. Her eyes burned through his skull. Nick looked okay. He had chosen banking as well. He was a few years older so maybe he was past that naïve 'I'm gonna make it big' career phase. And he was such a bore he might have actually genuinely chosen it.

"I guess that's why people have kids," Nicolas said, breaking the now slightly awkward mood. "To leave something behind, I mean."

Hugo chuckled. "Your kids are not you."

"Sure they are," Nicolas said. "Literally, since they're carrying your DNA."

"You are not DNA. Your kids are completely separate entities from you. It may feel like they're part of you now when they are young and they need you to survive, but they grow up, you know. They become individuals, independent, with separate identities and separate lives, who won't even call you more than once every third month while you are rotting away at some old folks home. Even that precious bit of DNA will be bred out of your bloodline in a just few generations. And after you're gone you won't be sitting on a cloud somewhere watching what that little stain of yours has accomplished with the chance at life your cum squirt gave him. You'll be *dead*. The idea that we live on through our children is an illusion."

Silence. They both stared down their now empty glasses and looked both angry and uncomfortable. People don't like it when their lives are being called pointless.

The situation was relieved when Lardy came down to their corner and offered a refill. The rest of the evening went in a lighter tone. Movies, work, politics, the usual stuff. When they left, that little piece of line crossing seemed all but forgotten.

**3**

The crisis was deepening. From one week to another the organizational levels outside FastCredit UK, those in New York, went completely silent. Hugo had a lot of reporting that went directly to them and when these normally quite demanding pencil pushers didn't call in for a while, Hugo decided to play dead. He stopped sending them reports. If the silence was permanent he could let go of that part as well. He never heard anything.

*How important can these reports really be if nobody even reacts when they stop dropping in?*

Bernie called those levels in New York *The Adminisphere*. A Brazil-like bureaucracy where the paper shuffling and decimal moving was taken to new heights. Bernie said that it had probably all been blown away in some desperate restructuring to cut costs. No such thing had been announced to Hugo's knowledge, but he too was sure that was what was going on.

Hugo still produced everything on his list that went to the local management, even though he didn't have a boss yet. But the disappearance of the 'adminisphere' gave him a lot of free time. The week crawled by without Hugo having anything to do. To make the days seem shorter he emailed friends, drank coffee, shot the breeze with coworkers and browsed around the internet. The internet is exceedingly boring in a bank. Everything is blocked by the URL filter. No Facebook. No Twitter. No games. No nudity. No nothing. It was like the Christian Right had designed it.

Today was Wednesday and that meant after work at *The Tick*. He always looked forward to that. At five he packed up his stuff and swung by Nella to see if she was ready to go.

"Go on ahead," she said. "Meet you there." Nella always had something extra to do right before it was time to clock out (figuratively, of course, there was no actual clocking at FastCredit). Always. Hugo didn't have that even back when there *was* stuff to do.

The place was packed as usual. The interior was empty, with everyone crowding outside the way British people seemed to prefer it (despite the cold). Lardy still always placed a reserved sign on their table in case someone suddenly developed an inclination to sit there. He poured a beer as soon as he saw Hugo in the doorway. "On me," he said.

"Really?" Lardy nodded. They had an arrangement with Lardy that he should never feel forced to comp their drinks just because they were friends. Everyone insisted on paying, so when he did treat you it was from the heart, not because he felt he had to.

"You look like you need one."

He did.

Nicolas arrived. There had been some light snow

and he was brushing it off furiously, as if it was napalm. The jacket was suede.

He had brought Bernie and Benzo. They were not usually part of their after work gang, but every now and then they both joined in.

"Still shitty at work, Hugs?" Nick said after taking a sip of beer.

"Not really. Nothing to do now for a while."

Hugo followed Bernie's example and ordered fish and chips. Lardy made the best in town. Naturally, given his proclivity towards deep fried food.

"Fat people enjoy credibility when it comes to cooking," Hugo said. "Lardy certainly lives up to it."

"That's a stereotype," Nella said. "Not all fat people like food. It can be genetic."

Nicolas and Hugo just laughed at her. Bernie and Benzo were a little more reserved, but they were both smiling. They weren't that familiar with the banter.

"Or it could be glandular," Hugo said, smiling.

"Or hormonal," Nick said.

"Or maybe they're just big-boned."

"Fuck you!" Nella said.

Nick turned towards the bar. "Lardy, remind us why you're fat again."

"I eat too much," Lardy yelled.

"You sure? You're not just big-boned?"

"No."

"You have a glandular problem or something?"

"No."

"Why do you make the best fish and chips?"

"Because I'm a fat bastard. I eat too much and I know food. Is it Nella again?"

They all nodded.

Nella gave them the finger.

Benzo ordered nachos. He was finally back in action after another one of his many sick leaves. He was now fighting to catch up with the IT issues that had gone unattended in his absence (something that was guaranteed to stress him out and lead to another sick leave, which would lead to more unattended IT issues and...). He could use a little alcohol.

Benzo validated all the stereotypical preconceptions one would have about IT people. He was still youngish, thirty something, ponytail, tall and thin with aviator style goggles and was always wearing Iron Maiden t-shirts. Everything about him screamed Microsoft in 1978.

His real name was Dennis Reardon, but nobody called him that. Benzo came from the complicated word *benzodiazepine*, a class of narcotic drugs used to treat anxiety and insomnia. Benzo had started taken them when he was still in his teens. It was his high school classmates who had given him his nickname.

"It's not me! It's the Xanax that makes me this way. You know, the benzodiazepines. The *benzodiazepines*!"

"The benzo-what-now?"

"Hey, Benzo! What's up?"

"Benzo! Benzo! Benzo!"

"I hated it for many years," he had told Hugo in confidence, "but after a while the name sort of stuck and I stopped caring."

Getting that benzo monkey off your back, Benzo had told him, would result in a stupendously horrible and protracted abstinence syndrome with crazy night terrors and panic attacks. Apparently it was nearly impossible to stop popping once you had gotten used to them. They were responsible for his many sick leaves, but only a few people at FastCredit knew that. The seniors and HR just thought he was 'prone to getting the flu.'

Benzo loved Hugo. He was the one of the very select few (maybe the only one) who had actually read anything Hugo had written without Hugo handing them the text directly. Many years ago, when Hugo had published that short story in Science Fiction and Fantasy, Benzo, who was apeshit for anything involving spaceships, laser beams and fake science, had actually read it. Ever since then he was Hugo's only fan.

"What is the great writer working on now?" he asked as Hugo downed his last chip. Benzo asked that a lot.

"Nothing," Hugo answered. Every time he asked. He didn't write anymore.

"It'll come to you," Benzo said. Every time.

Hugo needed to take a leak. Some of that raw toilet doodling would cheer him up. Lardy encouraged people to doodle on the stall walls. It was an art form, he said. Gave the place character. There was no censorship so some stuff could be really rough.

There was a now classic stick figure comic strip penciled on the wall of stall number three, above the bowl. It had been there for a few years.

The two stick figures had a conversation:

*'The one who's the most blasé about internet porn when he dies wins!"*

*"Last night I saw a black tranny with a cock the size of a*

*cricket bat, with a piercing through the frenulum, try to fuck himself in the ass with a melon!"*

*"What kind of melon was it?'*

When he came back out he changed the subject. He didn't want to talk about his writing. He'd even talk about work as long as his failed writing career didn't come up. He had to. It was the only thing they all had in common the times when Bernie and Benzo tagged along.

"I have some goodies on management," Bernie said after Hugo had strong-armed them into a work conversation.

Everyone took a sip and leaned in. Nick too, even though he worked for a different bank. Bernie was known for always having inside information about everyone and everything. Nobody knew how he obtained such information and he guarded the secret with the same fervency as an illusionist who refuses to divulge how he got the damn bunny down the hat.

"I heard rumors that they approved the Visa Zoo project," he said. "Remember?"

They all remembered. Hugo was aware of the approval, but not of any details. Hugo and his former boss were then ones who kept it 'a project' and not an actual product.

"What's that?" Benzo said. "Sorry. I'm just tech support. I don't keep up with that stuff."

Bernie chewed his food frenetically, obviously grateful that Benzo didn't know, and impatient to start telling. The Zoo project was one of his favorite bitch topics.

"It's a new campaign where the customer can combine his Visa card with a membership to the Zoo here in London. Just like your gas station card has a Visa symbol on it. Get it?"

Benzo nodded.

"You'll be able to see the commercial on TV and online pretty soon," Bernie continued. "According to the rumors our slogan will be 'Visa Zoo, turns you into a wild animal on the High Street'."

"We actually thought it was a joke when we first heard it," Hugo said. "It wasn't."

"Why is this bad?" Benzo said. "I think it sound pretty cool."

Bernie continued. "Well, in exchange for us getting to put our brand together with Visa and London's finest animal prison, we would get to buy their customer database for a reduced price so that we could sell our shit to them. Still expensive as hell, but still not as much as it would cost otherwise."

Bernie took a sip of his beer. He held up his hand to signal that he wasn't finished.

"And here's the best part," he said, almost while still swallowing. "As it turns out, the database didn't contain a single potential customer for us. Just kids, senior citizens, young people with no jobs, or temps and such. All of them with less than impressive credit ratings. They might as well have bought the Superman Fan club register. In summation, we spent millions without any chance of getting anything in return."

"Aren't you being a little unfair?" Nella said. "It was impossible for them to know that the database was unusable. If that's even true. It's just rumors, you know."

She gave Bernie a hard look. "Who's your source?"

"I have my tentacles out."

Nella gave him a sour look.

"I gotta hit the head again," Hugo said, and left for the bathroom. "Yeah, yeah. I know. I have the bladder of a twelve year old girl."

When he came back out it was Benzo's turn to regale everyone with stories of management screw ups. Mostly IT related ones since this was his area.

"They're too old for computers," he said. "They don't get that almost all problems can be solved by simply restarting the machine. Someone should write a book about what idiots they are!" He looked at Hugo.

"What?"

"You should write it! You're a writer."

"*Was* a writer."

"What?"

"I used to write. Past tense. Now I groan from just sitting in front of a word processor."

Nicolas giggled.

"What?"

"Groin. You said groin."

"I said groan. Real funny there, Beavis."

*Beavis and Butthead. Now there's an antiquated pop-culture reference!*

He doubted anyone under the age of thirty even remembered them. Or knew that MTV used to be a music channel once, for that matter.

"Real mature," Nella chimed in, but Nicolas was laughing. They were obviously getting drunk. She turned to Hugo. "Just take it easy. You just need to focus hard on your work and it'll be fine."

47

The others kept talking but Hugo floated away, thinking about Benzo's comment about writing the book. It wasn't exactly what he written before but an absurd story in an office environment could be fun. Maybe with a serious theme baked into it? Like *Scrubs* in a bank?

The idea was wonderfully appealing and Hugo felt a chill down his spine just thinking about it. The feeling was the same one he had had back in his early twenties, when his mind was ripe with grandiose and crazy ideas. Before Office-slash-Couples Hell had crushed his soul.

*Why not?*

He could write it during office hours, now that the crisis seemed to have taken away all his real work. If he could find a way to do it without getting caught, that is.

"I have to go now," Nicolas said. "Anna is visiting the grandparents with the kids this weekend. I have to help her pack, apparently."

"Wait, wait, wait," Hugo said. "You're not going?"

"No."

"And you have to help *her* pack! Pussy whipped." He made the sound of a cracking whip.

"Whipped!" Nella said.

Nicolas gave them the finger. "I can't leave work early on Friday. They're leaving around lunchtime. But I get the house all to myself for the entire weekend."

"So it's just you and internet porn then? Find some low quality tube and just stream away, huh!"

He flipped them off again.

"Nothing to do, then?" Nella said.

"Actually, my parents are coming. They're staying until Sunday."

"Awhh. Little Nick can't manage a weekend alone? Needs his mommy."

Again, the finger. But it was all in good fun. Hugo knew he hated when people called him Nick so he sometimes teased him with it. It was Nicolas. Nothing else.

"Why don't you guys come?" he said. "Bring Jessica too." Hugo and Nella were pretty tight with Nicolas's folks. They had spent countless nights at their house during their college years. He hadn't seen them in ages. Jessica had never liked them, though. She'd never liked Nicolas and Nella either, for that matter.

"We'll have dinner, send them to bed and after that we'll have the house to ourselves. It'll be like old times again."

Nicolas made a lot of money. Anne too. More than he and Jessica did. Staying with Chase had paid off in the long run. Their house was in Beckenham, well outside the underground system. There was National Rail, but Nicolas would probably drive.

"I'll go," Nella said.

"I don't know," Hugo said. "I don't know if I really want to relive the glory days. It's not time yet. Wait another ten years or so. If I haven't killed myself before then for still working in a bank."

"Come on! Don't be such a buzzkill. It'll be like the good ol' days as long as we go into it with a positive attitude. We'll laugh our asses off to Airplane. You know, Robert Hayes. Drinking problems. Leslie Nielsen. We'll drink, party like when we were in college. But with more expensive whiskey."

"And you are sure your parents won't mind?"

"Mind! They'll love it. You're like a son and daughter to them."

"Okay," he said, doing his best to sound eager. It was true. Nick's parents had functioned as a substitute for his own from whom he was sort of semi-estranged. His parents could never really accept that he wanted to live a childless life over in Europe.

"Benzo? You're welcome too," Nick said.

"No, thanks. I got other stuff."

*Yeah. Like a life, maybe?*

"Okay. If you change your mind let us know."

"Hey, Nick!" Hugo said, now that token inviting Benzo was dealt with. "As the only proud owner of a car in this company, you have honor of coming to get us."

"Noooo!" Nella said. "No Pat Benatar in the car. Pleeeaaase! I'll die."

"What?"

"You really don't know do you?"

"Don't diss Pat Benatar. How many times do I have to tell you?"

Hugo held out his hands in a mock gesture of apology. "No, no. My bad. She rocks. Everybody knows that."

The Pat Benatar thing had started out as joke. With Benatar's relative lameness and all, how could it be anything else? It was during their sophomore year in college; they played *We Belong* over and over to symbolize their increasingly symbiotic friendship. Pretty soon real emotions got attached to the song and when they all realized that it was too late. Now it was a staple, an eighties-new wave-delayed-synthesizer riff-reverb-on-the-drums-kind of monster, insisting on showing its ugly face every now and then, impossible to kill completely.

The night was coming to an end and everyone started making their way home. Nicolas took a taxi. He had been given permission by Anna to do that every after work Wednesday so he could ditch the car and have a drink.

"How do you get to work in the morning if you don't drive?"

"Taxi to New Beckenham and then the train to Tower Bridge. But I'm allowed to go by taxi all the way home in the evening."

"Lucky you."

After Nicolas left he followed Nella to the bus stop. She never took the Underground after dark for some reason. She kissed his cheek and gave him a hug before she got on the bus. When she was drunk she always got a little touchy-feely with him. He liked it. They were kind of 'opposites attract' sometimes.

On the Tube he thought about Benzo's idea. It wasn't a bad one. Just the thought of writing a book about the inadequacies of the management during working hours was exhilarating. Screw them out of a few paychecks. It was unconventional. Even vengeful. FastCredit was packed full of ideas for whacky characters, just waiting for someone to write about them. He grabbed an old newspaper from the seat across him and started scribbling ideas. He needed a plot. And a strategy for writing undetected.

**4**

*Stranger than fiction. Isn't that the expression?*

Hugo's new boss's name was Frank T. Rex. At first Hugo thought it was a joke.

The T-Rex! Like the dinosaur. That was simply his name from now on. When he later turned to be a grumpy old man with a huge rod up his ass and a pea-sized brain who screamed at people for nothing at all, it fit even better. To top it all of he was married to Layla, the head of marketing, but they had different last names.

*What is her name?* He couldn't remember.

It was the topic of the day, of course.

"I guess there's no mystery as to how he got the job, huh?"

"You think he was bullied in school for the T-Rex thing?"

"Why doesn't he just remove the T?"

"Maybe he doesn't see it?"

"Maybe he likes it that way?" Hugo didn't think so. The T-Rex didn't strike him as the kind of guy with a sense of humor.

Hugo pondered these questions while going on a

scavenger hunt to the kitchen for some coffee and a piece of fruit, if there was anything left. He had never been a big breakfast eater and always needed something to fill the void in his stomach around ten.

The fruit basket was new and still had plenty in it. Management must have forgotten to cut down on this kind of luxury when they chainsawed last month's expenses. Bananas, pineapple, and red berries of some sort filled up the basket. And apples. Astrakhan, Granny Smith and Golden Delicious. Hugo didn't know fuck all about apples but there were always little stickers on them with information about what kind they were. The other fruit didn't have that.

*Why is that? What's so fucking special about apples? Pineapple supposedly makes your cum taste better. What do apples do?*

A true apple aficionado eats apples with a knife. Someone had once told him that. He was right. He went over to the drawer and fished out some half dull knife and cut himself a piece. The automatic espresso maker had spat out his coffee. His sweet, caffeine-laced coffee that honestly tasted more like sulfuric acid than anything else.

He walked slowly back to his cubicle. As lazily as possible. He thought about the contrast between The T-Rex and Natalie. He was both saddened and disappointed. Nothing was right anymore.

The T-Rex was a walking bank cliché. One of those gray and balding gentlemen you see on the news, squirming and sliding past questions about extravagant bonuses and salaries while the company was firing Average Joe Bank.

*Or the average Smith and Jones? What was the expression in the UK?*

The T-Rex was a self-serving opportunist. A douche, quite simply. The new dictatorship was characterized by everything from registration of arrival times in the morning to micro-management tracking of any activity that took place during the working day. Home office days had to be approved by him personally (in writing), mail traffic was monitored by the requirement to have him copied in on everything so that he could 'keep up to date with what was going on'. Any analyses were to be signed off by him, even if it was really outside his area of expertise. Total surveillance. Orwell would have spun in his grave.

His old boss had been his opposite. She had always given her employees a lot of leeway and never looked over their shoulders. When she did put her foot down she was never a douche about it. You always felt respected and valued around her. She had been open to other points of views than her own, and could at least entertain the possibility that she didn't automatically know what was best just because she was the boss. A rarity in Hugo's world.

*Acceptable quality.* She had always used that phrase about the work. She knew the banking world was all superficial and phony and that nothing you did really had to be exceptional. Just acceptable. *Exceptional* was for other lines of work, like surgeons, academics, firemen, police officers. People who were responsible for stuff that actually mattered.

Frank T. Rex had made his mark already the first week when he tore the head off a poor assistant in Marketing (who didn't even report to him) for having the balls to point out an erroneous technicality in a marketing campaign approval that everyone else had missed. Rexie had final approval and had signed off on it with the error still in it.

"You will not come to me and accuse me of making an error without PROOF!" He had screamed so loud all of Back Office had heard him. He had jumped up and down, all red faced like Yosemite Sam. Hugo had seen the event up close and he thought he had even seen a tendril of saliva shake loose from the corner of his lip as he ripped the assistant her new asshole. Hugo had consoled her afterwards. It didn't help that she'd been right. She called in sick the next day and didn't return until the week after. As far as Hugo knew, The T-Rex had not even got a little slap on his fingers. Why would he? He was higher up in the chain. Justice, banking style.

More incidents followed. Of less caliber, but still. Hugo concluded quickly that it was a pattern rather than isolated events. The guy was a tool, pure and simple. He couldn't handle deviating opinions or criticism. Hugo had managed to stay clear of his wrath so far but he knew it wouldn't last forever. He hated his type. They would clash sooner or later.

"How's it going with that new boss of yours?" Bernie asked later at lunch.

"Meh. So far I've only done what I did earlier. But all the rapports I send him come back with a buttload of changes."

"Really?"

"Yep. So much so that he might have just done the report himself."

"Did he say he was going to do that?"

"Not in those words. I tried sending some older stuff just to see what would happen. You know, claim it was a mistake if he noticed. He didn't. He just erased what I had written and replaced it with his own comments."

"What does that mean?" Benzo said.

"That I don't have *anything* to do here anymore. The analyses was the job. But the T-Rex doesn't seem to get that."

"Sounds like you're getting Dilberted," Bernie said.

"Dilberted? You mean sidestepped?"

"Hell, yeah. For Frank, or The T-Rex as you call him, and for the rest of the management group you are a leftover from the past. You represent that calm cautious ideology that Bryce wants out."

"So that they can bloat the portfolio with customers that look good in the short run but will drag us down later? Later, when Bryce has moved on to some other job and won't get blamed for it?"

"Exactly," Benzo said, even though he probably didn't fully understand what they were talking about.

"That sounds about right, doesn't it," Bernie continued. "The T-Rex is a castrated little sycophant they hired so that there would be no uncomfortable questions."

"Makes sense. You know, at first glance they appear to be really stupid, but they aren't, are they? It's all very well thought out. They're evil geniuses."

"Evil, sure. Geniuses, I don't know. Maybe." Bernie took a sip of his water and gurgled it around before swallowing. "I guess nobody is going to call them on it. The people in power are all in on it. It's what they all do. Ratting someone out would be ratting yourself out. It's just the way this business works."

"Aren't you going to say anything?" Benzo said. "About the T-Rex, I mean?"

"I guess. I just don't know how. Or when."

"Well, I guess you have all the time in the world to think of something now that you don't have anything to do anymore." Bernie spit out a piece of pizza into his hand and put it on the side of his plate. "Gristle in the bacon. Yuck."

"He'll probably find something else for you to do," Benzo said.

"I don't think so. He doesn't want me involved. Not in anything that matters, anyway."

"Weird."

"Very."

Nella sat down next to Hugo. She often took a late lunch. It was part of some health drive she was pushing, which included eating many times a day but small portions. She ate twice before lunch. Carrots, apples and such. It wasn't working. She had two really big and greasy pizza slices on her plate.

"Fuck you," she said before anyone even had the time to make a remark. "So what's up?"

"Frank," Benzo said. "Apparently Hugo doesn't get along with him."

"No! Really! Who'd have guessed? In what way?"

Nella probably meant that Hugo was the problem, not the T-Rex. Nella. Always agreeing with management. She still trusted them, still assumed they were telling the truth and that they could guide everyone through whatever problem was at hand at the given

57

moment. Maybe it was her career ambitions talking, or maybe she was really blind.

"How do you work with a guy like him?" Hugo said. "He has a different frame of reference for everything. How do I get along with someone that has more in common with Principal Skinner than Bart? A guy that's never seen a single episode of *Friends*. A guy who never fell in love with Princess Leia in her gold bikini in *Return of the Jedi*? Who never fought to hold back the tears when Optimus Prime died? Who thinks *Seattle* is only known for the Space Needle? A crossword solving, Trivial Pursuit playing geezer who thinks that all *U2* songs sound alike while claiming that the *Stones* went through a fundamental change in sound between *Satisfaction* and *Rainbow*? The entire thing is condemned to failure before it even gets off the ground!"

"Ahh," Nella said. "He's old. That's the problem."

"Yeah. He's old," Benzo said.

Hugo nodded. "Exactly. I hate old people."

Bernie smiled. He was an old geezer compared to most other people here. When Benzo realized what he had said he looked away, as if he was ashamed of himself. "Not that *all* old people are like that."

"No, I am old," Bernie said.

"No, no. Just a little..."

"Don't sweat it, Benzo. I'm kidding." Bernie gave Benzo a reassuring pat on the shoulder. You had to be careful with Benzo. He could get really down on himself if he thought he did something wrong.

"Reception-Gina likes him," Benzo said. "She said he has a really great sense of humor. 'A little dry, but spot on', those I think were her exact words."

Hugo and Bernie looked at each other and then back to Benzo, who put out his arms as if to say, *don't look at me!*

"I'm just repeating what she said," he added.

"Gina only says that because she has no sense of humor herself," Bernie said. "I've talked to Frank and I can verify that he has absolutely no sense of what's funny and what isn't. I think he has learned somehow where to insert punchlines in a conversation to make people laugh, but it doesn't feel genuine. You know what I mean?"

He stuttered a little, trying to find the words. "It's hard to explain but you can see in his eyes he doesn't really understand why what he says is funny. He understand that it *is* funny, but not *why*. You get it?"

"Dead center," Benzo said.

"Couldn't have said it better myself," Hugo said.

"The result is that 'dry wit' Gina is talking about," Bernie finished.

He got home before Jessica. So it had been since the T-Rex had taken over. Before it had always been the other way around. Hugo had never had anything against working long hours as long as he knew it was worth it. The new order did come with some perks. It was nice to have their cramped London flat to himself.

He poured himself a whiskey and threw his feet on the table. It was nice to be able to do that without getting the look. He turned on the TV, chilled with *The Simpsons* for a while. He hadn't done that much in the last few months.

Hugo liked being by himself sometimes. Their activities—Jessica's yoga, his running—were almost always planned to take place at the same time. That way, Jessica said, they didn't waste precious *together-time*. In the beginning when they were still in the puppy love phase it was a no brainer to plan it like that. Was it still?

When she came home they ate dinner and Hugo aired his problem with the T-Rex.

"He's riding my ass about everything, even though I don't really have anything to do. When I arrive, when I leave, how long my lunches are, what I'm doing even though he's the one not giving me anything to do! It's a paradox."

Jessica replied by bouncing the responsibility back to himself. Or that's what he thought she did.

"Don't be so stubborn," she said. "Just do what he says. Why can't you just play along for once? I know some people are idiots but just try to play nice. Please? For me?"

"Don't know if I can."

"Why do you always fight to ruin everything?"

"I don't! I'm an individualist. Always was, always will be. And I don't take cock up my ass. I never will."

She gave him a sour look and fell silent. They had had this conversation many times. They were both sick of it.

"He's the problem. Not me."

They finished dinner in relative silence and then she went off to her yoga. Hugo decided to skip the jogging tonight and just chill in front of the TV.

The next day Hugo had finished what little he had left to do by eleven. He spent the rest of the day online, sending emails, texting and talking on the phone with Jess and Nicolas. Time crawled by. But five o'clock came eventually and Hugo prepared to leave for home. A little earlier than most others. The T-Rex wouldn't like it.

Before he left he talked briefly with him about the changes he had made in the reports and asked him how he wanted things to be going forward.

"What changes?" the T-Rex had said.

*Well, that was weird! Just denying it flat out like that.*

On the one hand it was good. It meant he didn't have to put that much time into the work anymore. It would give him time to write. On the other hand, it was still his work in the eyes of everyone else, including the seniors who read the reports. If the reports were fucked up he would be held responsible for them, not the T-Rex. He was sure this was going to bite him in the ass sooner or later.

## 5

"I'm writing it," Hugo said, "On company time." There was an full spread of baked goods on the coffee table Bernie had went to town on with systematic precision.

He turned to Bernie. "I just don't know how to hide it from the T-Rex? And from everyone else, for that matter."

Bernie gestured wildly with his arms as if he wanted to say something. He was working hard on giant bite of cinnamon bun, both cheeks bloated like Dizzie Gillespie trying to play with a cork in his trumpet. Bernie was never self-conscious about talking with food in his mouth (in front of co-workers, probably not in front of *the ladies*) and this time the bite was just humongous. He swallowed heavily, cleared his throat and took a deep breath.

"You have come to the right person," he said after swallowing part of the bite. "There are tricks." He had a childish mischievous look about him now. And a really, really wide smile. He took turns smiling and chewing.

"Okay, I'll bite. What tricks?"

When he finally had worked through the entire bite

he went on. "Easy now. Let's take it from the beginning." He cleared his throat again, this time in an exaggeratedly melodramatic way. "Let's see. You want to write your novel during working hours, correct?" He was enjoying this. "You want to do it undetected, correct?" His voice returned to normal. "The trick is to make it look like you're working in a normal manner while in reality you are *not*. For this purpose there are several different devices you can implement. Things, let us say, I have picked up during my twenty or so years of slacking off in this business."

"Why don't I have a problem believing that?" Hugo said. "Tell me."

"*The Jacket Trick*."

"The jacket trick?"

"That's right. *The Jacket Trick*! Here's what you do. Get a jacket, like the top of a suit kind of jacket."

He cleared his throat again. That cinnamon bun seemed to have gone down the wrong way. "When you're not on an errand or something you hang the jacket on the back of your chair. What everyone doesn't know is that the jacket never leaves the office. When you leave in the evening the jacket stays on the back of your chair. In the morning it's still there, making it look like you're already in, but maybe temporarily away or something. The jacket will work *for* you. In reality you're either home or locked away in some conference room working on your novel."

The cinnamon bun had finally settled down. Bernie leaned forward and eyed the rest of the pastries. He held a finger up, signaling that he wasn't finished. He started chewing on another one.

"Mmmm. Good." He chewed it thoroughly, like he was making love to it, all the while holding his finger up. Hugo was sure he milked it intentionally. He reveled in it, playing the mentor. A really weird kind of mentor.

"*The Jacket Trick,*" he continued while licking chocolate off his fingers, "gives the office slave the freedom he needs to work with whatever he wants. It looks like he's ambitious and always there at the office. It looks like he's in early and leaves late, every day, while actually he's home working on his novel until eleven in the morning and leaves at three to continue."

Hugo smiled. Could it really work? When he thought about it, that was exactly how Bernie used his jacket.

"That's not all," Bernie said as if he read Hugo's mind. "The jacket trick is the foundation but it works best together with other things. It's the *combination* of different tricks that makes you look busy at work. For example, always carry a paper in your hand when you leave your desk, but you know that one already.

"Mess up your desk. Hard working people always have messy desks. Pull out all your books, put Post-its in them with notes. It doesn't have to be real notes. Nobody will read them, trust me. Print all emails you receive. They look official and work-related. Spread them all over your desk. Pile them up.

"Put more Post-its everywhere. On your screen, on the edge of your desk. Write important people's phone numbers on them. It will give everyone the impression that you're important, which in turn will indicate that you are busy. A messy work station is key number two."

"Wow," Benzo said.  "You've thought a lot about this."

"Sure.  Why do you think my desk looks the way it does?  I hate working in an office.  I count the minutes every day until I can leave this shithole.  But I make my life a bit easier by slacking off.  It works.  As long as you understand it requires planning and creativity."

That afternoon Hugo went to H&M to buy a jacket. He found one that had a reasonably classic cut.  Navy blue, what else?  He had enough suits and jackets already, of course but he wanted to get a new one.  It was symbolic.  It would mark the start of something new, so why not splurge?

The following day he started putting Bernie's tricks to the test.  Jacket on the back of his chair, messing up his work station, mails, post-its, policies, manuals, anything printable went on the desk.  He even took a step further and messed up his Windows desktop, copy-pasting shortcuts all over it in a random pattern.

He took it easy with the writing at first.  Partly because he was still working out a structure and partly because he wanted to see if the illusion worked.  After a week or so he actually did notice how his co-workers started commenting about how many hours he was putting in, how he left late every day and was in early every morning.  Even the T-Rex seemed happy, or at least less displeased.

It felt gooooood!  As if something was about to happen.  Like he didn't just tumble around in a pointless existence with nothing to do anymore.  And he had to admit, he felt all good and righteous when he thought about how every hour he worked on the novel instead of his real work he would be cheating FastCredit and those evil bosses out of the salary they were paying him.

*They deserve it. Yeah, BITCH!*

**6**

*Why the fuck did I agree to this?*

It was time for the nostalgia evening at Nick's place.

Jessica was extra annoying because she had misplaced the top of her Chanel. Nella was coming, so she had to break out the big I-am-prettier- than-you guns. Just like *he* hated Will and Sarah, *she* hated Nella and Nicolas. It is the natural order of things to hate each other's friends from before the relationship started. Jessica had probably looked forward to a quiet weekend alone with him, under a blanket, watching some silly rom-com. Under the circumstances that would probably be preferable.

"You haven't washed it, have you?" She refused to let it go.

"What? The Chanel? No."

"It's hand wash only, you know."

"I didn't wash it!"

When it came to her clothes he only washed according to very specific instructions. He tried to be a modern man and take initiative with the household chores but sometimes it was just plain better to wait for orders. Like with clothes from overrated fashion brands.

"So it's Nicolas, Nella, us and Nicolas's parents? Why is Nella coming?"

"Really? Of all those people you think Nella is the one out of place?"

She didn't say anything and just kept sulking like she always did when she was angry.

While she was running around looking for her Chanel, Hugo was thinking about how to break it to her that he was going to write about FastCredit. He had come to the conclusion that there was no way to tell her without getting into all kinds of shit.

He had tested the waters a little bit and hinted to Jessica that he maybe wanted to change jobs. To do something more *meaningful*. He didn't mention writing. She always went apeshit when he did that.

"Meaningful jobs don't pay any money," she said. Cynical, but she was right. If they wanted money, working in finance was his only option.

"Money maybe isn't everything?" he said. She gave him a patronizing pat on the head as if to say 'dream on'.

They had both created financial barb wire around their lives that was very hard to break through. Money was important whether he liked it or not. Mortgage and expensive habits made it so.

He was hardly the first office slave in history who had dreamt about *doing something else*. Everyone does that. Only a few ever make reality of those dreams. Most of the time it just isn't possible. The sacrifices are too big. He would wait with telling her about the book plans until he had a more tangible strategy worked out.

It was time to go. Nicolas was honking his horn furiously down on the street. Hugo felt a desperate need for one of those *perseverance drinks* Bernie always went on about. He poured a quick whiskey and chugged it. Not the classiest way to go about it but it would have to do. Jessica had found her Chanel (he hadn't washed it) and was touching up her face. Another five minutes and they went down.

Nicolas had already picked up Nella and she was riding shotgun.

*Good. Then she and Jess won't have to share the backseat.*

Pat Benatar was on as promised and they were both singing along. *Weeeeeeeeeeeeeeeee belong!*

So it went. All the way. They were off key too.

The Smiths, Nicolas's parents, were old school. His dad had worked in the docks until everything was moved to Asia in the Eighties. After that he started working for the union, trying to preserve whatever was left from being shipped overseas as well. He was a pure blooded, socialist, anti-capitalist, Thatcher-hating Labour voter. And yet he managed to be oddly conservative when it came to family values. Get a good job and raise more Labour-voting offspring.

He had only a few years left until retirement and it was exceedingly difficult to get anything out of him that didn't involve pension schemes. Especially now that the crisis on the stock markets was chewing it all up. Nick's mom worked with the unemployed. Something bureaucratic. She was younger and a little more relaxed with pension stuff. But just a little.

Just like Hugo himself, Nicolas was the journeyman—the first in the family who had earned a single credit at a college and thereby officially broken out of the working class. A fact his parents were endlessly proud of.

It's funny how working class people are always so proud of who they are, and at the same time they cry tears of joy when someone manages to crawl upwards in the social hierarchy. Seemed contradictory to Hugo. Nicolas always told his folks it wasn't such a big deal to go to college today. It didn't require any particular talent, but higher education is something special for that generation.

When they found out that Nicolas's mom would cook for them they had stopped and bought some chocolates as a token of appreciation.

"Something to chew on for coffee," Nicolas said. "If they don't constantly have something to eat they'll only want to play Monopoly or some other boring board game. A high blood sugar level keeps them away from madness like that."

She had made pasties, a traditional pirogue-like dish that was the south of England's answer to the burger or something. Good stuff. Dough, meat, onions, potatoes. Fatty and salty. How can you go wrong? The only way it could be improved was if they deep fried it. *Anything* is improved upon with a good fattening deep frying, isn't it?

"How's work?" Nicolas's dad said. His name was John. (His name actually was John Smith, which of course drew suspicious looks from the concierge every time he checked into a hotel with his wife).

"Hugo has some problems with his boss," Nicolas said quickly. Probably to avoid having to answer any questions himself. Hugo's problem became the preferred topic of discussion for the entire dinner so he had achieved what he wanted.

"What?" John said. "Have you done something wrong?"

"He has reorganized things and moved most of my tasks to himself," Hugo said. "I don't have much to do anymore, except simple stuff like filing and copying and the like."

"So now he just surfs all day."

"Surf? The interwebs, you mean."

"The web, Dad. Or the internet. Not both. And not plural."

"Oh. Of course. So he wasn't happy with your work?"

"I guess not." He tried to keep it short. No need to go into it too deeply. The corporate sycophant theory that Bernie had would probably not fly with anyone here. Banking was also like most other jobs, filled with esoteric bullcrap that makes everything sounds more complicated than it is. No point in turning the dinner into a seminar.

John went on. "You must have done something if such a thing happens. Otherwise he wouldn't have done that. You kids. You have to work harder. Then you'll get somewhere in this life. Look at me and Christine. We worked hard all our lives. We're not millionaires but we can still count ourselves among the lucky ones."

Hugo felt a raging need to point out that their situation couldn't depend on hard work and luck at the same time. If everything was just a matter of lucky coincidence then what was the point of working hard? He made an effort to suppress that need. No point in inflaming things.

He looked over at Nicolas, who was also cringing at that comment. Nella, however, seemed to listen with sincere interest.

"I've started looking for a new job instead," Hugo lied. Better not mention any book writing plans in this company. The Smiths thought any kind of artistic expression was a waste of time. Artists don't make money and can't support families.

*But they do tend to vote to the left.*

"I suppose you can look for something else but that's the problem with you kids. You give up too easily. You quit your jobs, you divorce your spouses. All at the first sign of trouble."

"Dad!"

"It's true!"

"Maybe it is, but can we please talk about something else?"

"Sure."

The rest of the dinner was spent talking about musicals, TV shows, vacations and all that sort of idle chit chat. Boring, but way better than the third degree.

"Sorry, didn't mean to bring it up," Nicolas said after dinner.

*Yeah, you didn't! You got exactly what you wanted, you fucktard!*

Hugo just let it go. It was better that way. He

seemed sincere, though. He probably hadn't counted on his dad going at it with such fervor.

*Forgive and forget, I guess.*

Nicolas went back to kitchen to help his mom with clearing the table. Hugo and Nella went outside and sat down on the veranda. It had electrical heaters so it could be used almost the whole year around. The garden was in immaculate shape despite still being rather cold out. Spring was lazily approaching but Nick was way ahead of the seasons.

Hugo could never see himself having a garden like that. To him it would just be another prison, an anchor that limited his freedom of choice to change his life whenever he felt like it.

"You okay?" Nella asked.

"Yeah," he said while admiring the greenish shimmer the lawn produced in the dusky light. "I'm always okay. You know that. It was probably inevitable. Good to have it out of the way, I guess."

"Maybe he has a point? Maybe you're making your relationship with Frank more complicated than it is? Have you talked with him?"

"Frank? Oh, the T-Rex! Not used to calling him by his real name. I actually have a meeting with him tomorrow. He called it himself, not me. Maybe I'll bring it up then."

"Do that. I'm sure it'll work out."

"I kinda like Benzo's idea of writing a book about all the crap that's going on at FastCred." He decided to throw in a little test. Nella would perhaps be more open minded to the idea.

"Are you serious? Of course you are. You always

were a dreamer. By the way, what crap would that be?"

"What crap would that be? Are *you* serious?"

"So we're having a tougher time than before. Some people are stressed. Big deal. Everyone is doing the best they can."

"Do you really think that management are doing a good job?" He retold some of Bernie's gossip from their lunches. He shouldn't have to. Nella had been there for a lot of it. She not only defended management, but also the entire concept of a bank like FastCredit, whose whole business idea was to loan money to people who really couldn't afford it. She described it almost like it was a good deed. Like FastCredit was a charity or something. Everybody gets to hop on the credit train, even the poor.

"I guess it sounds egalitarian at first," Hugo said, "how big a favor have we done them when they can't pay back?"

Nella didn't reply.

Jess came out and sat down. Banking and finance wasn't really her favorite topic of discussion at social events (despite the fact that she was a controller at IKEA) so she changed the subject.

"Nice blouse," she said to Nella. "Where did you buy it?" Nella didn't like talking about fashion and clothes, he knew that since way back. She dressed nicely but she was of the opinion that you didn't have to have fashion as a hobby just because you're a girl.

"It looks like a Versace I have," Jess continued.

"Well, this one I bought at H&M," Nella replied.

"Oh. It really does look like my Versace."

Hugo wondered how many more times she would

74

say *Versace*.

"We should get together," Jess said. "Check out each other's wardrobes and have coffee or something."

At first this comment confused Hugo. He would've never believed that Jess would want to spend time with Nella but he soon understood that Jess never really had any intention of actually seeing her. She wasn't interested in her wardrobe. No, this was about something else. Women, in his experience, never say what they really mean. He couldn't figure out what exactly was this was about, though.

"Sure," Nella said, not exactly bursting with joy.

"We'll get in touch later." Jess would never be in touch.

The discussion ended when Christine brought the coffee out. John had a bottle of whiskey in his hand. He poured a glass for himself, Hugo and Nicolas.

"What about me?" Nella said.

"Oh. Sorry. You girls usually don't drink the horse piss. I forgot that you do."

"Yup. Nella's a cowboy," Nicolas said.

John poured another one. Jess and Christina had a glass of white. The conversation quickly slid over to movies again, which in turn transformed into the Smiths' patented improvised movie quiz. It was a spectacularly geeky tradition of theirs that they used to torture any guest they had.

John usually led the way with a pop-quiz on old baby-boomer favorites, and so he did this time as well. He started off with a thorough run through of his old school macho heroes. Steve McQueen, Ben Johnson, Sinatra and of course his namesake John Wayne. Who lobbed a bullet to hit a baddie in *The Magnificent Seven*? James Coburn, but he was really aiming for the horse. Who played the drunk in *Rio Bravo*? Dean Martin. What was Billy the Kid's shotgun loaded with in *Pat Garret and Billy the Kid*? Sixteen thin dimes. They had heard it a thousand time before when they hung out here as college students.

"Okay, my turn," said Nicolas, who didn't seem to be as ashamed of his old man anymore when he took off like this. They all got caught up in it. Except Jess, of course. She thought this was childish nonsense, if he knew her like he thought he did.

"Same spirit," Nick went on. "For you, Hugo. The four main stars and the director of *The Iron Cross?*"

"Please," Hugo said. "Is that all you got? Coburn, Maximillian Schell, David Warner and James Mason. In no particular order. The director was Peckinpah. I've been here enough times to know any movie Coburn's ever been in."

"Yeah. That was too easy."

"My turn," Hugo said. "Something a little bit more modern. Hudson in Aliens? The second movie."

"I hate that modern crap," John said.

"Nobody knows?"

Christine didn't know. She never did. Jess shook her head and shot Hugo annoyed looks as if she wanted to communicate her disappointment that he even participated.

"I know," Nicolas said. "Michael Biehn."

"Ahhhh... so close."

"It was Bill Paxton," Nella said. "Michael Biehn played Hicks."

"Okay," Hugo said. "Somebody else? Jess? Name a movie?"

She shot him the most ominous look yet. She held it half a second too long to be comfortable. *I'm sick of this now. Bitch, bitch, bitch.*

"No thank you," she said. "I'm not really that interested in these kinds of games."

The sleep-over never happened. Jess wanted to go home. Nicolas offered Nella to stay but she thought it would be weird with just the two of them (even if Nicolas's parents would be there) so Nicolas drove everybody home. Jess didn't say a word the entire trip home.

At home the silence continued. When she was in that mood Hugo always tried to punch a hole through the irritation by chit-chatting, telling jokes, tickling her, anything to try to make her laugh. The irritation usually passed after a while and she would start chatting back. Eventually the smile came and then everything was back to normal.

It didn't work this time. Jess's magazines always bitched about never going to bed angry at each other (Hugo read them sometimes while he was in the can). This time she obviously thought an exception was in order. Hugo had to admit the magazines had a point. It didn't feel good.

*What a fucking disaster.*

The evening had proved to him that trying to relive past eras wasn't an answer to your troubles today. Pat Benatar didn't work anymore. The Eighties reverb-on-the-drums monster was truly dead this time. They didn't *belong together* anymore. It all just felt really weird. He promised himself he wouldn't fall into the nostalgia trap, whining about his problems while nostalgically dreaming about the past. Too many people do that already. He needed to go forward. He needed to write that book.

**7**

Monday started with the entire building having to be evacuated. FastCredit and the other companies residing there had to leave their offices, and emergency services had to come and clear the building before anyone would be allowed back in. The rumor was that a higher up in FastCredit had been smoking in the basement and accidentally set off the fire alarm. Layla, the head of Marketing, was both a smoker and had been implicated in similar events in the past. The same thing had occurred at least once a year since Hugo had started working here. Nothing could ever be confirmed, of course, but FastCredit had to pay the bill for the emergency services.

The rumors also said that Layla wasn't just smoking when she triggered the alarm. She hadn't been alone down there. A young guy from customer service had been down there as well. He didn't smoke.

Maybe that didn't say too much but Layla always wore slightly too revealing clothes and that, together with previous rumors about little romantic get-togethers, of course resulted in the conclusion that naughty things had been going on.

Hugo normally didn't make too big a deal about rumors, but with everyday reality of working at FastCredit quickly becoming more and more bizarre he didn't perceive it as impossible. None of Layla's romantic transgressions had ever been proved but such confirmation was rarely necessary in the office world. Rumors equals truth here.

When he was back up it was time for his talk with the T-Rex, half an hour delayed because of the evac. It was half past eleven and Hugo thought this was the best time to interact with him. He had noticed that the T-Rex didn't eat lunch. He actually didn't seem to eat anything the whole day except a piece of fruit every now and then (oddly enough, the T-Rex seemed not to be a meat eater). At this time he had just chowed down his banana or whatever he chose to stuff himself with. His blood sugar would've reached its peak for the day and his morning grumpiness would be gone. If you couldn't reason with him now, you probably never could.

"Come in and close the door," he said when Hugo showed up in the doorway. The T-Rex went over to the panorama facing the hallway outside and closed the blinds three quarters, just enough so that you could see what was going on outside but you couldn't see in.

The T-Rex's desk was neat and clean, with everything placed in perfect angles. Stapler, hole cutter, ruler, fancy expensive pens, all placed in a perfect row. No stacks of papers, no books. Just a picture of The T-Rex himself and Layla. No kids. Layla's kids were all from a previous marriage.

Layla was younger in this picture. She sort of reminded Hugo of Candice Bergen, back in the day, of course. Hugo couldn't help but wonder what a woman like that could possibly see in a man like Frank T. Rex. They were definitely not on the same level physically, and considering what Hugo knew about what was on the inside of this anal retentive douche, she had married down.

They took their seats. The T-Rex just sat there in his chair for a long time, looking at Hugo, his arms in a trapezoid shape in front of his chest. A deliberate power position, no doubt. He rubbed his palms together, like an evil genius in a cartoon just before he breaks into the typical *muhahaha*-laughter. Hugo could've sworn he had raised his chair a little too much, probably to make him seem bigger and overwhelming. The T-Rex had been taking management classes, that much was sure. He focused rather intensely on Hugo as if he was trying to stare him down. Hugo wasn't deterred. Instead he had trouble holding back a big belly laugh.

"I sense things aren't well between us," the T-Rex finally said, his voice very soft, kind of apologetic. "I can't say that I am happy with your work here, Hugo. Your analysis hasn't gone over too well with the rest of the management team."

*What did I say? Didn't I say this would come back to bite me in the ass? I think I did.*

"I've taken some heat about them," the T-Rex continued, "but I defended you as best I could."

Hugo felt his facial muscles contract into an involuntarily smile. A sarcastic one, of course. Now that the rest of the management team was involved it really wasn't a laughing matter. Naturally, it could hurt him pretty badly if everyone turned against him. But he couldn't help it. It was just too outrageous, what T-Rex said.

"Is something funny?" the T-Rex asked, his voice annoyed now. Hugo had decided before he got here to stay cool and just see what the T-Rex had on his mind, but this was just too much.

"No, not funny," he said. "I'm not sure what's going on here but let me remind you of what has really happened..."

"I'm not interested in any excuses," the T-Rex said, now clearly angry. "I'm tired of these incidences with you. I simply don't have the energy to have these discussions every time we talk. You're going to have to raise the quality of your work from now on. That's all."

*What fucking incidences?*

He had brought it up only once! Hugo was baffled. He couldn't think straight. The T-Rex was either a complete maniac or he had the biggest balls he'd ever seen. Just lying like that, straight to his face.

*Un-fucking-heard of!*

The T-Rex went on. "I've heard from the others in the business that you are a swell trooper and pretty good. You haven't shown it so far but I'll give you another chance."

*Unbelievable. And 'swell trooper'? Dude, the Fifties called and they want their expression back.*

He just couldn't let this go. He had to call his bluff. Or his insanity or whatever you wanted to call it. Either way he wasn't going to take this quietly.

"I'm sorry," he said, "but don't I have a say at all? I have a different opinion about what is really going on here."

He knew the T-Rex couldn't handle it when someone disagreed with him, and it started to show. His cheeks were starting to redden in the same way they had with the marketing assistant. Hugo still went on.

"I sent *my* report to *you* like you asked. They came back with so many changes that they weren't even mine anymore! *You* changed everything. And then *you* took them to the management team. I can't be held responsible for them not liking a report that I didn't even write."

There. The bluff was called. It didn't matter. The conversation was already one of the stranger ones Hugo had ever had, and it just kept going. Like it was taken straight from the mouths of Yossarian and Major Major in Catch 22.

"Changed *your* report? Why would I change *your* report?"

"You tell me?"

"It's *your* analysis."

"It's not mine if *you* actually wrote it."

"Of course it's yours. *You* wrote it."

"But I didn't write it. *You* changed it."

"No I didn't. Why would I change *your* analysis?"

"You tell me?"

"But it's *yours*."

"It was mine but you took it over. Just like you took over the credit committee meetings."

"The credit committee meetings isn't *your* job."

"It used to be before you started here. *You* took it from me."

"Why would I take *your* job?"

"You tell me?"

"Your job is *your* job."

"What *is* my job?"

"You know what your job is."

"You've retracted my job description to make changes and I haven't got it back yet."

"But you know what your job is. Your job is what you do. Not what I do."

"*You* don't seem to know what my job is."

"Your job is your job. You do what I don't do. You don't do what you don't do. You don't know what my job is and what yours isn't. You will do what I don't do, but what you do, that which is not mine and those things that are yours!"

"WHAT! That doesn't even make any sense!"

By now the T-Rex's face was almost purple. He stood up now and gestured wildly with his arms. Hugo wasn't nervous or anything, like you can get when your boss verbally wails at you like that. He was just completely taken aback by the fireworks.

"You don't tell me what my job is. I tell you what yours is. I am the boss, not you. I don't take instructions from you!"

Now Hugo understood Bernie's comment about him looking like Yosemite Sam. His cheeks were almost blue and his lips moist with saliva. He was shaking like a druggie on his first day of rehab, his arms flailing all over the place. Just like when he had chewed the poor marketing assistant's ass off in his first week. Wow, what a show! He understood now why the T-Rex was so good at always getting what he wanted. Few people could withstand such a blast of madness.

"Enough now," the T-Rex said. "Go out and do your job. I expect better from you the next time." He went over to the door and opened it, motioning for Hugo to leave. He did.

Now he really wanted to strike back. Put that idiot in his place. Play a little. But how? How do you argue with a lunatic? He could go to Bryce or to HR, but that would only bring a whole shitload of official inquiries he didn't want to have. It would be a war he couldn't win. Managers always have each other's backs. The T-Rex would have to be handled with something else than logic and argument.

That day he had his lunch with Bernie and Benzo. Boeuf Bourguignon. Hugo never had really understood the point with that dish. It didn't taste of anything to him. Everything was boiled to point of being liquefied and it always seemed his body wouldn't absorb any nutrients from it. He was hungry again after an hour.

He retold the conversation with the T-Rex for both of them. They just shook their heads in disbelief.

"But not really surprising," Bernie said. "A lot weird things are happening here lately. I've always been fascinated with how ordinary gray office rats can flip out completely when the money stops coming in. When their jobs are threatened."

Hugo agreed. When everyone had plenty to do they worked together. But it was really just a quasi-solidarity that broke down at the first sign of trouble. Now that the stream of new customers was drying up, a lot of departments had a surplus of personnel. Hugo definitely started seeing clear signs of turf war and back stabbing. Nobody wants to seem out of things to do when the business starts getting stingy with expenses.

At the same time Nella and her colleagues in FinCon

had a hellish time with stress and long hours trying to piece together the semi-annual forecasts. Divides between haves and have-nots are never a good idea.

"Do you guys remember that we signed on for a bonus program about two years ago?" Bernie said.

"Sure," Benzo said. "About a month's pay if things went well, right? For managers and officers only."

"Exactly."

In all the turmoil Hugo had almost forgotten about it. He had never been paid anything.

"Anyone seen any money?" Bernie asked.

"No."

"Exactly. We should've gotten a payout for last year by now. Things were still good last year. But nothing. And guess what? I heard rumors that management just got theirs, or rather *gave* it to themselves. But everybody else got nothing, despite the fact they we had the right to some. And then we hear nothing about it. Not even a lame-ass excuse or something. Not even a tiny little note about how we failed to live up to some insignificant criteria, or some other lie. They just didn't care to inform us."

"Pure madness," Benzo said.

"It might even be illegal," Hugo said. "Breach of contract. Why hasn't any one of us said anything?"

"I brought it up with Bryce," Bernie said. "He said he'd get back to me. That was last month."

"Things like that always go to the back of the list in a crisis," Hugo said. "Management is panicking. They know that if they don't turn things around soon there will be consequences. New York will start calling in and they'll want to know what's going on."

The discussion went on. Bernie had more goodies on management screw-ups.

"There's apparently more problems with the Zoo-Card," Bernie continued. "Management wanted to withdraw from the contract once they found out that there was no profits to be made but they had missed a clause in the contract. One they wrote in themselves that said that the contract couldn't be canceled prematurely without both parties agreeing. They knew that but tried to cancel it anyway.

"The Zoo lawyered up, of course. Management had to apologize and then they tried to blame our own legal department for not telling them that the clause was there. That didn't fly, though."

"Of course not," Hugo said. "Playboss's signature is on contract. Just gives the impression that he's one of those idiots who signs stuff without reading it first. Too busy admiring his titanium golf clubs to have time for the fine print."

When lunch was over Hugo went straight back up and worked on the novel. He had started taking notes, documenting all that went on around him. Especially the kind of candy Bernie had just shared.

*Everything goes into the book from now on.*

All the idiocy and all the whacky people here just begged to get written about. All he had to do was to change the names of the guilty.


"I've started writing it now," Hugo said when he saw Nicolas and Nella on next Wednesday's afterwork at *The Tick*. "I have a few character sketches, a basic plot. FastCredit is a gold mine. Stupid people. Financial crisis. Intrigues, excitement, stress, pending unemployment for everyone. It's just made for dramatization. Everything that happens from now on goes into the book."

Nella slammed her beer down hard on the table. "I don't wanna be in some stupid book."

"Don't worry, you won't," he said with a smile. "You're not exciting enough for fiction."

"Oh, fuck you!"

"I did once, remember?"

"And as I recall you thought that was pretty exciting."

"Meh. It was good, in a vanilla sort of way. You know... good, but not mind blowing or anything."

She hit him in the shoulder. He tickled her back. They both laughed.

"Seriously, I don't wanna be in it."

"Don't worry. I'll make up most of the characters." A lie. It's almost always a lie, even in fantasy novels and shit like that. Writers always say they make it up but a lot of the times they don't, especially with goofy characters. You just change things around enough so that people won't get offended. Or even realize it's them. Management and the T-Rex would be in it, of course. Maybe others too, but he kept quiet about that. No point in antagonizing her further.

"I suppose I can see the point," Nick said. "But how are you going to do it? It takes a lot of time to write a book. Where will you find it?"

"Office hours," Hugo said.

"Really? How do you plan to do that?"

"I have nothing to do, remember?"

"Maybe so, but that doesn't mean you can use that time any way you want."

Nick had a point. Even if you have nothing to do it doesn't mean you're not expected to work. It is one of the most annoying paradoxes with life in an office. Even if there are layoffs coming and everyone is aware that there's nothing to do, you have play the game. Pretend you're busy. Otherwise there will be hell to pay.

"Besides, your boss seems to think you do have stuff to do," Nick continued. "He'll catch you."

"No he won't. I got it covered." He told them about the tricks Bernie had taught him. They weren't impressed. He could tell they thought it was wrong. Unethical.

"Like that's the most unethical thing here!" he said. "The whole fucking banking business is one big cesspool of questionable ethics. Cutting class when you don't have anything to do anyway is nothing."

That didn't bite. They both looked angry now. Nobody likes to hear they work in a filthy business. Better to pretend and rationalize. Tell yourself little lies to make you feel better. But he knew he was right.

"I know you're a dreamer," Nick said, "but isn't it time to finally live in reality for a while? Writing books is a romantic fantasy. It's indulgent. Sure, write some in your spare time. Have it as a hobby but don't mess with your job. Think about Jess. Sooner or later you'll have a family to support too. What are going to feed your kids with? Old drafts?"

"He's right," Nella said. "I wanted to move to Seattle and be a grunge-rocker, if you remember? We're not

89

twenty anymore. For Christ sake, we're even closer to forty than twenty-five. Time to grow up and take responsibility. Working in a bank isn't such a bad thing."

*Grunge-rocker!*

That wasn't a fair analogy. She wanted to be a *grunge-rocker* for three and a half months back in their freshman year while she was all hornied up for one of those weed smoking Bohemian types that every college has hordes of. She never even played an instrument.

It was clear he wasn't going to get any support here so he didn't pursue the subject any further. Nevertheless, he pondered their objections on his way home. He didn't want to let the boy who still lived inside him down. That boy didn't want to waste away in an office for the rest of his life. He was like the Little Prince. He didn't care about money, social standing or power. He just wanted to do the things that he thought were fun. He wasn't ready for the grown-up world's beige fetish for responsibility.

*Can't you have boyish dreams after thirty? Really?*

Hugo refused to accept that. He always would.

**8**

*It's weird how the mood of a workplace can shift that much over a single weekend.*

He walked around, visiting the different departments to find inspiration for the book, and maybe to see if anyone was in the mood for a chat. Gloomy doom was hanging over the place today.

*Everything goes into the book.*

It was all normal on the surface. Everyone greeted him just the way they always did, they smiled as usual, waved hello as if nothing was different. But it was. It took a while before he noticed the fear. It was in their eyes. Few could hide it. Nobody could escape it. The thought of losing your job and not be able to meet the car payments, pay the electrical bill, buying brand toddler clothes and video games for your money burning preteens so they'd keep quiet long enough for mommy and daddy to squeeze in a tired quickie, could drive anyone to silent madness.

*The malcontent is seething beneath the depths, slowly rising towards the surface to burst open in a tsunami of panic.*

He smiled to himself. He had to remember that one.

It smacked of literary pretentiousness.

*Not 'panic'. Too simple. Apprehension? Trepidation? No? Captain Thesaurus strikes again. Ah, screw it. I'll work on it later.*

When he returned to his seat he found a mail in his inbox notifying everyone that some people in the top levels in New York had 'moved on to new challenges'. Code for being fired. A monkey could figure that out.

*So it begins...Dumm, d-d-d-dumm, dumm, dumm, duuuuuummmm...*

He still needed to soak up inspiration so he went over to get Bernie. Perhaps they could grab an early lunch.

*Procrastination. The favorite hobby of any writer.*

"Feel it, Hugs?" Bernie asked as Hugo stepped into the cubicle. "Something is up today." He gestured with his hand as if there was some kind of electrical charge in the air.

Hugo nodded. "I feel it too."

They went down to the cafeteria to grab lunch.

"The high ups always lock themselves in their offices when things start to go south," Bernie said as they sat down; he checked around so that nobody could over-hear. "I've seen it many times during my career."

Now that Hugo thought about it, the seniors' office doors were actually closed today. They were usually open.

They served fish today in the cafeteria. Not the fish n' chips kind, but fancy fish with bones, boiled potatoes and sauce.

*Oh well. At least it won't be fish tomorrow then.*

(But it was. The cafeteria had goofed on their orders

and now had enough for the entire week.)

"The people in customer services don't seem so depressed," Hugo said, and told Bernie about his observations.

"Maybe not. They're young and stupid. Or at least uneducated. They don't keep track of what's going on in the world or know anything about economics. They don't read the paper and they live for Friday nights at the club. They have faith in leadership and expect the mighty to fix everything for them."

"Nobody reads the fucking paper, Bernie. It's the future now. Tablets. Internet. Smartphones. MMO's. Heard of them?"

"Ha! Good point."

Bernie chewed intensely on his fish.

"Yuck!" He drowned it in lemon. "I hate fish unless it's deep fried! I've never understood the point."

"But they must feel a little worried? The customer service people, I mean."

Bernie's face was now drowned in mayo and lemon juice. He even had to use the napkin. Reluctantly. He had pointed out many times that napkins just slowed down the eating. Only with *the ladies* did he take care to watch his table manners.

"Sushi," Bernie said, ignoring Hugo's question. "The day I eat sushi is the day Hell freezes over. I don't believe people really like sushi. If food has to be drowned in some fuck-all spicy sauce to even be eatable it can't be truly good. Wasabi, I mean. What the fuck!"

Bernie wiped himself again, and now seemed to be done with badmouthing the fish.

"Sure, you noticed the mood change," he said returning to Hugo's question. "I felt it this morning as soon as I stepped inside the door. Everything is quiet in some ghostly way. Like the spirit died but the body keeps breathing."

Hugo nodded.

"The terror will soon spread to middle management," Bernie said. "It might have done so already. That's why the T-Rex is so fucked up. He's just trying to survive, make *his* bosses happy and show them how much they need him. He doesn't know how to act when you are being a little obtuse so he flips."

"He doesn't want anyone else getting cred from the seniors without something sticking to him."

"Precisely."

"You know what? I feel watched in a different way lately. Not just by the T-Rex but by everyone."

"You're just nervous because you've started writing the book. That's all. You'll relax when you got some routine going."

"Yeah. I hope so. I might be a little paranoid right now but it really feels like everyone is watching me."

"I get it. Everyone gets paranoid in times like these. Just wait until they start firing people."

"You think they'll fire people?"

"I'm sure of it. It might be a while, but trust me, it's coming."

After lunch Hugo felt more watched than ever before. He was disappointed with how easily he got caught up in the game.

*What is she looking at? What does he know that I don't?*

He had to stop for a minute to shake it off so he could think straight. It was just like Bernie said. In bad times paranoia will blanket any workplace. If people in his surroundings got nosier it would demand much more from his illusion. Long hours in front of the laptop without doing any real work was something other than surfing around and running on fake errands. While doing legitimate work, his screen rarely displayed text and certainly not any organized in book form. Just spreadsheets, numbers and charts. He needed more tricks.

The day ended already around three with another evacuation (this time in the rain), again because of a triggered fire alarm.

*Layla again? The entire basement is riddled with no smoking signs!*

The entire staff was gathered outside again while the fire department was clearing the building. Hugo stood with Bernie and Nella just chit-chatting when The T-Rex and Layla came up to them.

"Gents," the T-Rex said. "Everything under control?"

*Gents?* He would be a guy to use such a word, wouldn't he? Gents! Rex was fluent in *lame*. Besides, Nella was a girl so Hugo guessed the greeting wasn't directed at her.

Everyone said hi. Nella too. The T-Rex turned to Hugo. "I am leaving early today to do some errands with my wife."

"Ahh," Bernie said. "Some quality time?"

"Yes. I suppose you could call it that," Layla said.

Layla was hot, no doubt about that. She had kids from her old marriage and was in the right age bracket.

The term *milf* applied.

*Age bracket? Great! Now I'm speaking lame.*

They all chit-chatted for a while. Cold talk about nothing. Hugo didn't know if he was imagining it or if it was real, but he found Layla staring at him on several occasions. The kind of intense look you give each other in a bar when you want to hook up. Every time he looked her way, her eyes were glued to him.

The T-Rex finally ran out of patience with the conversation and ended it. As the two of them walked off Layla turned around and threw one last look at Hugo. Did she wink? Hugo thought she did.

He got confirmation from the others as soon as the couple were out of earshot.

"Did you see that, Hugs?" Nella said.

"See what?" Hugo said, playing ignorant.

"Looks like you got yourself a little cougar there," Bernie said. "Did you see how she looked at you?"

"Yeah, I did," Hugo admitted. "What the fuck was that all about?"

"Better watch it," Nella said, and nudged him with her elbow.

"And why now? We've worked together for months and she hasn't done anything like that before."

"Don't go there, buddy," Bernie said. "It's something weird. Probably something that has more to do with Rex and her than with you."

"You mean it's a 'he works for my husband' kind of thing?"

"Exactly."

"Kinky."

They teased him for a while longer. It was okay. It

wasn't the first time a woman had shown him some interest.

It took the fire department an hour to clear the building and by then it was two o'clock. Hugo rarely stayed longer than three these days, so he thought he'd sneak out. He packed up his shit and left. *The Jacket Trick* would handle the rest of the day for him.

Life in an office consists of routines. You come, you go, you get coffee, you put the cup in the dishwasher (first you put it in the sink, then someone puts up a note on the fridge that says 'your mom doesn't work here!' and *then* you put it in the dishwasher), you send reports, you have meaningless Personal Development talks with your boss, you negotiate your salary, go to morning meeting, look at PowerPoint presentations (with bad grammar; finance folks may know numbers but they can't write for shit) and so on. If any of it is exciting it only lasts for a while. Everything turns into gray routine in the long run.

One new routine he actually liked was accompanying Nella to the bus (she refused to take the Underground - too much people, hot stale air, too dark, people with BO problems pressing up against you and so on). Today she had decided to leave early too, and they kept company.

Their friendship had cooled a little over the last few years after university and it was kind of nice to reconnect. They had a deeply rooted friendship that could take a little cooling off. One those that never dies and picks up right where it left off even if a long time has passed.

Their discussions were always interesting and that faint sexual attraction between them of course made the whole thing more interesting. She was cute but not the type of übergorgeous babe he was usually attracted to (he and every other guy, whether they admitted it or not).

"So you just left," Nella said when Hugo told her he hadn't notified the T-Rex that he took the day off.

"Frank thinks I'm working hard these days and lets me make those decisions for myself. Hehe!"

He counted on the tricks fooling him but he didn't tell her that. She didn't know about them and for now maybe it was best if she didn't.

"So, you're writing that book? What if they find out?"

"They can't object if they don't know about it."

"Sooner or later you'll get caught and it won't end well."

"So you're saying you're worrying about me?" He nudged her gently in the side with his elbow.

She smiled. "You'll lose your career."

"Don't worry. I know what I'm doing."

"Be careful. I'd hate to see you get into trouble."

"I'm a big boy. Not that I don't appreciate your concern."

"What is Jessica saying about it?"

"Nothing. She doesn't know."

"You're kidding?"

"No. I haven't told her because she wouldn't approve. And I definitely haven't told her I'm doing it during company hours. She'd freak out completely."

Nella stared at him. "That's not good, Hugo. Think about why you haven't told her for a second."

Hugo was aware that it had to mean something that he hadn't told the woman he was supposed to love about such an important thing. Damned if he knew what, though. Couples have secrets from each other, don't they?

"Do you really have to tell each other everything?"

"Maybe not everything, but this is big."

"Not that big."

"It's your life."

That's all the talking they had time for. The bus was coming. They said good bye and Hugo continued to the Underground. There were seats available this early in the day so he sat, but he didn't fall asleep as he usually did when he got to sit. He had some things to mull over.


The next day Hugo spent the entire morning writing. It went well. Bernie and Nella had had another heated argument about the crisis earlier and he wanted it in the book, so he pushed through while it was still fresh in his memory.

Bernie and Hugo always took their afternoon break around three. They usually took it in one of the kitchen areas. Many of the seniors had previously had that routine as well but not anymore. They probably had the coffee, but they stayed in their offices now. Today he found Nella there instead. Bernie had left early.

"I guess it's a pretty cool idea to write that book," she said. "I understand that it must be frustrating with Frank."

"Not really frustrating. I view it more as a challenge. Almost like a game, actually. It's kinda fun."

"Aren't you worried?"

"Sure. I can't afford to get fired. But it's better than the alternative which is to just sit here and pretend to busy. I'll die of boredom."

"Just don't make me out to be a bitch or something."

"Hehe. But you are a bitch."

Elbow in the side.

"I don't have a complete plot yet. Just some isolated stories. You know, about my old pal Rex and Management."

"Do you really think it's as bad as Bernie says?"

"Yes. The numbers don't look good. It'll be a tough ride."

"Maybe it's a temporary dip?"

"Dips are always temporary. There's always recovery on the horizon. Question is how deep the dip is and how long it lasts. And this one will be pretty deep and last a long time."

"And you don't think our management can pull us out of it?"

"No. They couldn't find ice on Greenland, let alone a way out of this."

Nella was quiet for a while. Hugo knew she had to start doubting by now. Why shouldn't she? She had access to same numbers Hugo and Bernie did. How could she not see it? Maybe she just didn't want to see?

"It's good you've started writing again," she said. "You've always been creative. Maybe banking isn't for you after all."

"Banking isn't for anyone," Hugo said with a grin.

Nella smiled but she was clearly annoyed too.

"I have to get back up," she said. "I have the account transfers to do."

"Ohhh. The dangerous spreadsheet. Don't screw up." He was teasing her. She gave him the finger. He kept teasing her on his way up. Eventually she loosened up and started smiling for real again.

That Wednesday the gang was together again at *The Tick*. No cameo by Benzo this time, though. He had decided to try to wean himself off the Xanax again. It didn't go too well so he kept away.

Hugo told Nicolas about his progress writing the book. Nick let loose his typical cannonade of skeptical remarks which Hugo tried his best to zone out. He had decided already and was well into the process. The pros and cons section of the project was long over and he wasn't going to turn back now. When Nicolas finally gave up they talked about everything and anything except work. Every one of them was sick of all the shit in the business. Even so, he felt pretty good. The everyday trudging had been broken up. The immediate future promised excitement. The book, the tricks. It seemed to lead somewhere. But he knew it could also explode in his face. Expectation, longing and anxiety braided together. It was a strange feeling.

**9**

In a few months he had developed the illusion from being a few random tricks into a complex network of lies and scams. His latest addition was music. He had brought an old web-radio from home, on which he played non-provoking easy-listening on a low volume. It was run on a timer and started exactly seven-thirty in the morning every day and ended at seven-thirty p.m., after everyone had gone home. It contributed to the illusion that he worked long days. After all, who plays music when they're not there?

Today he came in at about half past ten after first writing for two hours at home. Before entering the office space he went down to the basement where there was a locker room and a free gym nobody used. The risk of being seen there was minimal, and should it happen he could always lie that he was thinking about starting to use the facilities.

"Awh, you know...I'm over thirty now. Everything will start to get pear-shaped if you don't work out. Blah,

blah. You know, healthy diet, cardio, carbs, blah, blah."
Anyone would buy it.

He had hidden a stack of *important papers* and bogus files in a locker in the locker room that he could hold in his hand when he walked into the office. He had dumped his briefcase. Coming in with a briefcase in the middle of the day would be a giveaway that he hadn't been in yet.

"Mess up your hair and wrinkle up your shirt a bit," Bernie said. "You only have perfect hair and an impeccably ironed shirt in the morning when you show up. You have to make it look like you've already worked for hours otherwise you'll blow your cover." Bernie had considered every detail. Hugo had taken it one step further. He had stopped shaving and grown a three day stubble. It gave him a slightly ragged and overworked look. This was something Bernie probably wouldn't think of. He didn't shave because he didn't have the energy. Or wanted to. Or possibly because the girls liked the stubble when he was out booty hunting.

"It's important not to look too career minded. Look busy and stressed, but don't make yourself out to be career material. You wanna be left alone, not be promoted and get more work that might be more difficult to hide."

He kept sending The T-Rex old reports which he had simply put today's date on. He used current statistics, fresh from the data warehouse and just copy-pasted an old analysis. The T-Rex would just delete it anyway and write his own.

Anything else (like reports that went directly to New York before those people were swept away into oblivion) he sent he marked *For Your Information*. Hugo had learned a long time ago that it was completely risk-free to just delete anything marked with that. It required no follow-up. No one would quiz you on it or ask you to actually do anything. Everybody else did the exact same thing. It was the first time he had found that label even remotely useful.

When he finally was inside the office walls he swung by the T-Rex's office (with all the *important papers* in his hand) to remind him of all the stuff he had sent him but that it wasn't urgent that he look at them. He made small talk to keep a friendly atmosphere brewing and then he went to his chair and started writing.

To make the illusion even more authentic he rumbled around in the mess he had made for a while as if he was looking for something. He added some angry remarks and curse words every now and then and made sure those around him heard it. He shook his head and seemed generally in a pissy mood. It was a type of theater he had learned from *George Costanza* who had slid through nine seasons of office work in *Seinfeld* without doing anything. Angry co-workers are frightening. Nobody wants to risk getting into a conflict so everyone just stays away.

Writing session number two for the day he completed by his desk. He had to be seen in his cubicle sometimes, otherwise it would cause suspicion. He kept a spreadsheet ready in the background, ready to be alt-tabbed to the foreground in case someone should decide to pop their head in.

The illusion worked. It looked like he had exactly the amount of work on his plate that he wanted the T-

Rex to think he had. The novel was taking shape. Characters were born. A plot was outlined. He had even written a few pages of the manuscript itself.

Later that day he was called into the T-Rex's office. He went in there with great confidence, convinced that the illusion was working.

"We've had a tough time," the T-Rex said. "But I feel that it has approved lately. What do you think?"

Hugo agreed. It *was* better, but not for reason the T-Rex thought, of course.

"I'm glad you think so," the T-Rex continued. "Nobody thrives when you have a bad relationship with your manager. Your attitude is clearly better. It feels like you've finally accepted me as your boss and gotten started on your work."

Those kinds of comments still pissed Hugo off. Part of him wanted to argue. It took real effort to remind himself that the plan was to write. The book was everything. The T-Rex was a douche and deserved to be brought down and he would get his at some point, but not right now.

"Yes," he simply said.

"It's understandable if it's hard to adjust to new circumstances but you'll push through eventually," the T-Rex said. There was a smug happiness to his voice. He had won, he thought. "It's not always easy to get a new boss who wants things differently. Besides, the situation in general is a little tense here at FastCredit. It can be hard."

Hugo nodded. He thought it was best to just say as little as possible. That way he would avoid saying the wrong things.

"Let's put it behind us," the T-Rex said. "And to show you I hold no grudge I have a special project for you."

Hugo froze. The last thing he wanted was new things to do, especially not tasks with measurable results like a project. Projects had a beginning and an end, usually resulting in a tangible output that could be reviewed and judged. It would break the nice status quo he had achieved.

He looked at the T-Rex with eyes that he hoped would signal expectation and curiosity. He had to demonstrate interest. The illusion required it. That the T-Rex had put their quarrel behind him was a victory. He had gained the man's trust and that was a very valuable commodity. It would mean continued leeway, continued freedom from prying eyes. It was imperative that he didn't undo that.

"Sounds exciting," he lied.

"I want you to prepare the entire business for the big audit coming later this autumn." The T-Rex smiled. "Bryce has given me the assignment to arrange it and I thought it could be an exciting task for you."

Hugo screamed inside. Preparing for an audit basically meant you copied and put papers in binders according to the audit department's specifications. Stuff they would later scan for errors with a magnifying glass. He couldn't believe how many rungs on the corporate ladder he dropped since the T-Rex took over. The assignment was basically secretarial work you'd delegate to people way down in the food chain. He wanted to argue again, but clenched his jaw. It didn't matter anymore.

*The book! The booooook! That's all.*

It would be incredibly time-consuming work to collect all the materials and it would undoubtedly steal time from his writing, but he thought he would be able to manage it.

"Wow!" Hugo said as enthusiastically as he could. Probably not entirely convincing. It didn't have to be. The T-Rex knew that Hugo would consider this beneath his station. That was probably the entire point. To show him who was in charge.

"A lot of work," Hugo continued. "I'll gladly take it."

"Great," the T-Rex said. "Just talk to me if you have any questions."

*It could've been worse,* he reminded himself. It would be time consuming but not very complicated. However, it was a very concrete task and would be hard to dance around. When the audit came all that material just had to be in the binders, but he had plenty of time and could probably milk it for a while. Hopefully it also meant he could avoid any additional things being shoved onto his desk in the meantime. His plan was still alive, albeit in need of some changes.


Lunch again. Fried pork of some kind.

"One of my faves here in England," Bernie said.

"Yup. It's one of the better things in the British cuisine."

"It's gross," Nella said.

Men like fat meat dishes, women like salads. A cliché that was often true. Then again, FastCredit was filled to the brim with clichés that were true.

"It must be hard being a girl," Hugo said.

Nella nodded. "Sure. We have to give birth to children and yet we have to stay slim. We get raped. We only get eighty percent of men's salaries and we are cut out from the highest positions in government and business."

"I didn't think you were such a feminist," Benzo said.

"She's not," Hugo said. "She's just bad at conveying sarcasm. Another thing girls don't know how to do, BTW. Sarcasm."

Elbow in the side. Hard this time. He nearly lost his breath.

"That clear enough?"

Hugo nodded and exchanged a mock 'she's an idiot' gesture with Bernie and Benzo. "Sure," he said. "I take it back."

It had become a habit not to sit with the others at one of the big tables. The previously tight community that normally characterized FastCredit had been broken up into smaller informal groups. The seniors sat by themselves. Before they had sat with their staff. The front office staff kept out of the way but the spirit within the group still seemed strong. The analysis geeks in Financial Control didn't want to mix with analysis geeks from Risk Management.

Nella was the exception. She was Finance and had no problem sitting with Hugo and Bernie who were Risk. Naturally their personal relationship outweighed any cracks in workplace moral. Otherwise, who knows what would have happened? Benzo had always avoided everyone except Hugo, Bernie and Nella.

"We're having visitors next week," Bernie said.

"Three big shots from New York. They're here to talk to the management team."

"About what?" Benzo said.

"I don't know, but I'm guessing it has to do with our numbers."

"Sure," Nella said. "It has to be."

"Does that mean you have accepted that our management is a big crap pile of idiots?" Hugo asked. Nella gave him the finger. As a joke, he thought, but he was still sure there was a fraction of seriousness in the reaction.

"It's just getting worse and worse," Bernie said. "Nobody can deny that."

"It is," Hugo said. "We're in trouble."

"Look for another job kinda trouble?" Benzo asked.

"Probably. If you can find one in this economy."

"Someone's going to get the blame for this soon," Hugo said, "and it won't be anyone in management." It would most likely be him, he knew that. The T-Rex would blame him to save his own ass, no question.

"Screw it," Bernie said. "You have your book now. How's it going?"

"Good," Hugo said. "I've created a couple characters and a rough plot."

"What exactly is it about?" Nella asked. "FastCredit is the inspiration, you've said that already, what's the story going to be about?"

"It's about an analyst who's sick of his job and decides to write a book on company time about how their idiot management drives the bank into the ground. All the while he creates an illusion that makes it look like he's doing real work while he in reality is writing his book."

Benzo laughed. "Just like in real life!"

"You're kidding?" Nella said, and looked at him like he was an idiot.

"No. I'm not kidding. The guy in my book is writing the same book. The character he's writing about is writing the same book. It's like holding a mirror up against a mirror. The same reflection repeated infinitely."

"Huh," Bernie said. Hugo wasn't sure if he liked it or not. "Let me read some when you got something finished."

"Me too!" Benzo said. He was smiling like a little kid at the carnival. "It's soooo cool that you're writing again."

Bernie was chewing madly on his pork. "Mmmm. Salty. I see you've invented some new tricks too. The music was a nifty little idea. Wouldn't have thought of it myself. But I have another one for you. I did it in the Ninetiess. During the crisis in the early Nineties."

He chewed for a while. It was obviously a particularly fatty piece of pork. He made faces. Hugo couldn't tell if he was enjoying it or if it tasted bad.

"It involves lunch," he said. "We won't be able to eat together anymore for it to work. That's the downside."

"That's a shame," Nella said.

Benzo nodded.

"We'll talk on our coffee breaks instead."

Hugo nodded. The lunches were nice but with the T-Rex's 'special project' weighing him down, he needed some extra ammo.

"It's pretty simple," Bernie said and gave up on the

pork. He spat it out into his hand and placed on the rim of his plate. Gross, but less of a torture than watching him chew for all eternity.

"Excuse me," he said and continued. "This trick is called *the half eaten lunch*. Take something from home. Leftovers. Something that stinks, garlic or cheese or something. Make it clearly noticeable. Heat it up in the microwave oven here at work and place it on your desk and just leave it be. After a while you take your laptop to an empty conference room to write.

"Everyone in the office will think that you've run away somewhere on an urgent errand, so important that you didn't even have time to finish your lunch. Nobody knows that this lunch is never actually eaten at all."

There were a few people here that actually did that. They, of course, had completely legitimate reasons for not having time to finish their lunch but nobody needed to know that Hugo didn't. Perfect cover.

"Leave it there for the rest of the day," Bernie said. "It'll remind everyone that you're busy as hell and they'll leave you alone."

"Brilliant," Benzo said.

Nella shook her head. "You're both sick."

"We know!" Hugo and Bernie said at the same time.

"I'll buy it," Hugo said. "I'm starting tomorrow."

"Don't do it every day. Two, three days a week, otherwise someone will notice the pattern."

Hugo nodded. Bernie was a genius.


The following weeks went without incident. Everything was peaceful and quiet. The seniors stayed in their offices, blinds closed. They rarely undertook any forays out into the cubicle landscape and if they did, it certainly wasn't to motivate the now chronically depressed staff. It was a deceptive calm, Bernie said. He called it *the eye of the storm*.

He had started coming in an hour earlier to do some actual work on the audit. The modified routine seemed to work without any hiccups. After that he continued with some writing, first in his cubicle, then in a conference room where there was less chance of being disturbed. All his tricks were in full effect.

After a while the T-Rex started to want updates on his progress with the audit. It was only to be expected. Hugo lied and said he was halfway there, but added that there was an awful lot of material that had to be copied and that it would still take a long time to finish. The T-Rex bought it but Hugo knew that sooner or later he would have to produce real results.

That Friday night he and Jessica went to a concert. The London Philharmonic was playing Berlioz's *Symphonie Fantastique*. Hugo had never been a big fan of classical music but he didn't dislike it either. Jessica claimed to like it but always seemed bored out of her mind when they actually went to a concert. He often found her texting or reading mail. She never played any classical music at home even though she had her laptop full of it.

Hugo was pretty sure she was in love with the *idea* of listening to classical music and the associations that came with it. It made her seem sophisticated talking about it, subtly belittling others for just listening to 'commercial' stuff. She was well read on the subject and talked about all the concerts they went to at parties, but never a single word about the music itself and what it did for her. Hugo found it amusing.

After the concert he asked her what she thought.

"What?" she said absentmindedly, as if she hadn't expected the question.

"Did you like it?"

"I guess."

"Anything in particular you liked?"

"All of it."

She changed the subject and started talking kitchen redecorations. She talked about Will and Sarah and their plans to redo their entire house once they had actually bought one. Now it was Hugo's turn to slip into a haze of nothingness. The rest of the evening was just more of the same. When it was time for bed he was just grateful.

## 10

During the last few weeks Hugo had started to notice an increase of requests from the T-Rex in his inbox. It was always something insignificant or downright unnecessary, like double checking some numbers or a formula in some spreadsheet. He never found any mistakes and why should he. All the spreadsheets and formulas they used were ready-made by experts in New York and had been checked there both once and twice before they were sent here. The tasks were spot checks meant to test Hugo.

When the T-Rex asked him one late afternoon why he never was at his desk, Hugo took it as confirmation that his habits had started to interest him too much.

"I'm often out helping other departments with their reports," he said. It was true that in the past he often toured the office helping others with such things, but now most departments had simply stopped attending to that particular part of their jobs. Hugo had never bothered to ask why or escalated it to management. It would have just meant more work for him and less time for the novel.

The T-Rex had bought his lies, if barely. Hugo put on his jacket and did a quick symbolic tour just in case the T-Rex would actually ask around if he had been there.

"Sure. He was here," everyone would say. They wouldn't go into detail since they didn't want to be implicated in any lapse in the reporting themselves.

The small quasi-tasks he received were at least easy to handle. They just went out with return mail with a simple 'OK/Hugo' in the subject field. Once or twice he added a longer comment to lend it all some credibility. He knew the T-Rex wouldn't do a follow-up since the tasks were make-believe from the start. The T-Rex knew they were, of course. He was the one making them up.

After the tour he threw the jacket back over the back of the chair and left to write some more. Conference Room Two was all the way in back of the office and at this time it had no projector. That meant you couldn't run PowerPoints so the room was seldom used. That in turn meant Hugo could work in relative peace there. Should someone enter the room he would just tell lie about needing to get away from the buzz of the cubicle landscape for a while. Everyone could relate to that.

He had trouble getting started, though. This week was the week when he was going to tell Jess what he was up to and his mind was constantly preoccupied with devising strategies. How was he going to put it? He had come to the conclusion that there was no way Jess was going to take this with any kind of acceptance or understanding. She was going to freak the fuck out. He had made reservations at a French restaurant at Covent Garden. Some luxurious pampering before divulging the truth would soften the blow.

*And by blow I mean the shit storm that's gonna rip my face off when she hears what I have to say.*

Wine would help a little. He made an effort and put the thoughts aside, and he actually got some writing done.

After about an hour Benzo came knocking. It was okay. Hugo needed a break.

"How's it going? he asked.

"With the writing or with the T-Rex?"

"Both."

"I think he's on to me. He's probably noticed I'm not here too much in the mornings."

"That's bad."

Working hours were relatively unregulated at Fast-Credit. You could come in late in the mornings if you liked (within reason, of course, which Hugo completely ignored). As long as you compensated by working more at some other time. It was one of the few things Hugo still liked about FastCredit.

"It's very bad," Hugo said.

"I can imagine," Benzo said. "I've noticed that he often swings by your place around nine. You should know that."

The T-Rex had made it clear from the beginning that he didn't like the kind of flexibility in working hours that FastCredit employed. Eight-thirty sharp! Not a minute later. Hugo's trick had been to send a few fake reports from home at that time to clock himself in without being there. The T-Rex of course knew he had remote access and it was just a matter of time before he understood he actually wasn't at the office when he sent them.

"I need something else to make it look like I'm here in the mornings. I'm doing the Jacket Trick and the music trick but it's still not enough to complete the illusion."

"The screen," Benzo said.

"Exactly. It's blank in the mornings since my machine isn't turned on yet. A blank screen wrecks the entire illusion."

"Leave it on when you leave in the afternoon. I know it's against the IT security policy but I'm the one who enforces it. I won't tell. I promise."

"Will it work? It still goes blank pretty quickly after you stop working and the panel where you can change it is locked."

"I can fix that for you. I have administrator privileges, of course."

"You won't get into trouble?"

"Nobody has the time check up on me anymore. No controls or anything."

"Just what happened to me as well."

Benzo nodded. "Exactly."

The adminisphere slaughter was cutting across the company. Nobody escaped it.

"I'll fix it so the screen never locks," Benzo continued. He smiled widely. "Also, take some screen shots of the applications you work in. You know, your spreadsheets and such. Then use the Windows picture slide show screensaver and rotate the pictures slowly. That way your screen will always appear to show work-related stuff. Then you leave it on when you go home at night and the screen won't be blank in the morning when the others get in, but filled with spreadsheets. It'll look like you're already here and maybe just left your seat for a short errand or something."

Hugo could barely hold back the laughter as Benzo copied Bernie's inflection and body language.

"You're a genius, Benzo!"

"Oh, yes!" Benzo smiled.

"Thanks, Benzo."

Hugo always made sure he thanked Benzo properly when he had helped him with something. It was important for him to feel needed. They both went to Hugo's cubicle and went to work on the screen settings. Ten minutes later it was done. Hugo had chosen five images from the applications he worked in (or rather, should be working in) and it was ready to roll. The jacket, the music and the screen.

After lunch that day Hugo felt he needed a break. A real break, not just one of those fifteen minute ones with coffee in the kitchen. He needed a genuine change of scenery. He threw on his jacket, grabbed some important papers and left for the park.


The lunch crew today was just Hugo and Bernie. Hugo had an off day with his own little lunch trick so he took his food as he always had done. Nella was home with a cold and Benzo was busy with the installation of some new encryption software designed to keep intruders from hacking the bank's systems. It didn't go well. Marketing was first on the list to get the installation and a bunch of their machines had instantly crashed. But Bryce had still ordered the installation to continue. The problems would be ironed out later, he said. Hugo got a feeling Benzo would be busy for a long time.

"Danny Mac quit," Bernie said when they had sat down. He smiled widely like he always did when he had some good stuff on management. Danny Mac had been the Collections Manager and had only been with FastCredit for a year. Now PFHEET! Gone. Just like that.

"Really!" Hugo said. "Did he find something better? Or maybe you don't know?"

"Rumor has it he got fired. His numbers look like shit."

That didn't surprise Hugo. Everyone's numbers looked bad and if Danny Mac got fired for that, everyone was in trouble. Layla in Marketing was the only one who still had some control over the situation. They had of course canceled almost all marketing activity. Hard to lose money or suffer from spiraling costs when you don't do anything.

"I've seen it before in other jobs," Bernie said. "It starts with managers disappearing. Some leave of their own accord, others will have 'moved on to new challenges', as they call it."

"Then middle management, team leaders and analysts are next in line."

"Yup. But our people are usually included in some mass layoff, not on an individual basis like with poor ol' Dannyboy."

"So we got time?"

Bernie nodded. "You look a little distracted today, Hugs. What's going on?"

Hugo told him about Friday's dinner plans with Jess. Bernie gave him a pat on the shoulder. "It'll be all right, kid."

That half-fatherly concern actually helped a little.


At a quarter to five Hugo was still at his desk writing. Longer than usual. He had decided to stay for once, just to make sure people actually saw him at the office for a full day. The illusion required that kind of sacrifice every now and then.

This time it proved to be a lucky shot since the T-Rex was on him. He came out to his cubicle constantly asking pointless questions. Tiny little tests, like everything else he did.

"How much have you done on the audit project?" he demanded.

Hugo still hadn't done very much but of course he wasn't going to say that. He had counted on the T-Rex wanting to see the actual work sooner or later. He had just been hoping for later rather than sooner.

"Where are the binders?" he asked.

"I've collected them on a shelf in the big archive," Hugo said. It was a lie. He had collected about ten percent of everything in a plastic folder, now collecting dust in his bottom desk drawer.

"Can I see it?"

*Oops!*

"I haven't labelled the binders yet," he said. "It would be simpler to just wait until I have. You won't be able to navigate through the material without the labels."

*Way to think on your feet, Hugs! Sometimes I amaze even myself.*

"When can you be finished labelling them?"

"By tomorrow before we go home?"

That would be enough time, wouldn't it? Maybe put some fake binders up to make it look like he had done more and hope the T-Rex wouldn't go through it very thoroughly.

"Do it tonight, please. I need to know now."

*Crap!*

"It's not enough that I tell you my progress?"

It wasn't, of course. He knew that already but it was worth a shot. The Audit Head, or one the other ten or so bosses who had something to lose by angering the Audit Department, had probably put pressure on the T-Rex.

"Just do it, okay!"

*I'll shove that audit up your ass. Yeeeeaaaah! Beeeaaatch.*

"Okay."

The T-Rex was happy and returned to his office.

He had bought some time, at the most. Very little time. He'd never be able to put together the twenty or so binders it would take to satisfy the T-Rex in one evening. Then it struck him. The archive also contained last year's major audit. It was all there, neatly placed in binders. The same information that he had to collect now, only a year old. Hugo was thinking that the T-Rex wouldn't know the difference. He was completely ignorant about most of the material (despite making claims to the contrary).

Hugo simply printed new labels and put them on the back of the old binders. The T-Rex wouldn't see the difference. Maybe if he really looked carefully, but he wouldn't do that. He just wanted to see that something was happening.

Hugo didn't replace all of them. Just twenty or so to make his progress credible. He also selected binders with manual reports, like spreadsheet and database printouts. These were often not dated and wouldn't reveal his trick unless somebody actually crunched the numbers. If that happened, he would just tell a lie.

"Oh gee whiz. Something must have gone wrong. I will correct it!"

When the T-Rex came to inspect, he walked up and down the shelf with the binders. He eyed them intensely for a few seconds. He bend over to read the labels closer. He even touched one of them, as if to make sure they were real. He might have had a slight look of surprise on his face, Hugo couldn't really tell. In the end the T-Rex bought it.

"It looks good," he said. He didn't flip through any of them. The beauty of cheating big is that nobody ever expects people to have the stones to pull off something so ridiculously mischievous. It simply must be a mistake, a misunderstanding, an omission or whatever. There just must be some rational explanation other than that someone is scamming your ass off. The bigger the lie, the less people are likely to call you on it.

"You've done well," he added. "Since I held you here for a few hours tonight you can come in a little later tomorrow."

"Very kind of you," Hugo said, "but I don't have the time." Hugo recounted aloud all the work he no longer had. All the reports he no longer did. All of those the T-Rex *thought* he still did despite the fact that the T-Rex himself had taken them from him.

*Amazing! If I can just keep him clueless like this I might actually finish the novel sometime.*

Hopefully before he got fired for what he had done, or before FastCredit was blown away in the crisis.

The week finally ended and it was time for the dinner with Jess. He felt jittery, almost cramped up, from nervousness. Tight situations like this were usually not a problem for him. He cared for Jess. They had a good thing going and he was just about to break something to her that in *her* mind was bad news.

*Well, I guess messing with your livelihood is pretty irresponsible.*

They were mostly quiet, studying the menu. The appetizers came and they ate in relative silence, uttering just pointless pleasantries.

"It's good."

"Hmm. Yes, really."

"How's the wine?"

"Good."

"Busy week?"

"Yeah. You?"

"Yes."

He could see that she was uncomfortable, like she already knew what he was about to spring on her. Maybe she'd understand. Writing was his *mission*. His very purpose. His inner... something. Hugo didn't really believe in any kind of new age bullshit. Souls, destinies, predetermination, it was all fantasy. Life is just a series of rational choices. And sometimes irrational choices. Emotions are just chemical reactions in the brain, but he *felt* this. Intensely. The metaphysics behind the feeling didn't really matter. He couldn't let it go.

When the appetizers were done he told her. About his desire to keep writing, about the book, about using his job as inspiration, about writing during office hours, about endangering his job, his source of income. *Their* source of income.

"I knew something was up," she said. Her eyes were both sad and angry. "I thought we had been through this. So many times. We were going to put that behind us. Build a home. A family. You can't..."

"I'm sorry. I have to. I can't live without it. It's just not me."

"I get it. But life is long. There will be time for this later."

"When?"

"When we're older."

"Like when we retire?"

She didn't say anything. Even she realized that it was a long time to wait.

"It's not that I don't understand, but you've gone too far this time. If you lose your job we're screwed! They'll catch you and then we'll be out on the streets. We can't manage on just one salary. This is London."

"I won't be caught."

"What if you are?"

"I won't!"

She stared hard at him. The sadness was gone now.

"Just give it five years. Will you do it? For me? Then we'll see where we are. I don't want to wait anymore. I want a baby. I'm thirty five already. I can't wait any more."

"I can't. I have to do this."

Now her eyes were all rage.

"FUCK YOU, Hugs," she snapped, and splashed her wine in his face. Hugo was stunned for a moment, then for a second he was angry, then he realized what she had just done."

"I can't believe you did that?" he said. He broke out in laughter.

"Don't laugh at me, Hugs."

"I'm sorry," he said, still laughing. "It's just… that never happened to me before. I only thought that that happens in movies and shit. It was cool. I'm putting this in the book. Definitely!"

"This is not a joke, Hugs. This is our life."

They were loud now. The other guests were turning their heads, trying to gauge the situation without prying too much. Jess was becoming aware of this. She looked embarrassed.

"I'm going home," she said. She started to get up. "Don't follow me. I'll see you later."

"Jess, don't go."

She went for her coat.

"Jess! Jessie. Jesster. I'm sorry!"

She didn't stop.

*Shit. Fuck.*

He paid the check and left.

**11**

On Monday Hugo was still a little torn from the fighting with Jess. It had continued over the entire weekend. Finally they had agreed to let it go for now. A truce of some sort. They had had fights before, of course, but he couldn't recall any one being as bad as this one. It was so bad he even felt relieved to be at the office. That's saying a lot.

Nella was still out sick and Benzo's problems with the encryption software had escalated to new heights. The regional IT chief was now involved, and on site to try to limit the damage. Still nobody seemed to know exactly what had gone wrong. Benzo had yet again been forced to increase his intake of Xanax to stay calm. He was walking around the cubicle landscape like a zombie, mumbling to himself between meetings with the big IT chief.

Bernie and Hugo ate lunch alone during those days when Hugo didn't do his lunch trick. Hugo had had a quiet couple of days since the T-Rex had been away on a conference.

"Look!" Bernie said just after they sat down. "Layla is eating today."

"Seems like it. That's not something you see every day."

Layla usually had her lunch in her office. She had put two smaller-sized lounge chairs and a table in a corner and there she usually sat, mousing away at a small salad she brought from home. Hugo couldn't help but noticing her skirt was shorter than usual today.

"There's one of those in every office," Bernie said as if he read Hugo's mind.

"One of what?" Hugo said, pretending he hadn't noticed the skirt.

"A middle-aged, or at least soon to be middle-aged, woman dressing like a teenager, never eating anything but a salad, with ridiculously high heels, bleached hair, gliding around in the office with a seductive smile giving men dubiously flirtatious looks."

Bernie had been in the business for more than twenty years and he could possibly say something like that with a certain amount of confidence, although Hugo could remember such mature femme fatales prancing around from past jobs as well.

"Shit! She's coming this way," Hugo said.

Bernie suddenly became quiet and averted his gaze down onto his plate. Hugo was baffled, but amused to see that there were actually some women left in this world who could rattle Bernie's cage. Hugo was pretty sure there was no history between them, so it was something else.

"May I have a seat here, boys?" Her accent was distinctly British, her inflection always sexually charged, somehow.

"Sure," Hugo said. "Pull out a chair and park it."

"What are you guys talking about?" she asked, very tongue-in-cheek. "Football? Chicks?"

Bernie and Hugo stared at each other, both struggling to find words.

"Soccer," Bernie said. Of course he couldn't say what they were really talking about, but that was beyond clumsy. Neither Bernie nor Hugo knew much about soccer.

"Oh, yes," she said. "You Americans call it soccer. So, did you catch the England-Bangladesh game last night then?" she said.

Hugo understood from that comment that Layla didn't know anything about soccer either. He was pretty sure that was a cricket match. Despite that, they still spent the following ten minutes discussing soccer.

That's what social life in an office is like most of the time. Pointless chit chat about stuff nobody really wants to talk about, just to be civilized or for that matter, just to put up with each other.

When there were still fifteen minutes left of their lunch Bernie excused himself, claiming he had a meeting. It was a lie, that much was for sure. Hugo gave Bernie an angry look for leaving him alone with Layla. Bernie shrugged apologetically and mouthed, "I'm sorry." Then he left.

"So," she said, "just you and me then."

"I guess," Hugo said.

"So, how's it going?"

"Fine."

"Really? I heard you have some problems with Frank."

"You're a straight shooter," Hugo said. That was something he normally appreciated but perhaps not today. He had just planned to do some more small talk and then bow out. That plan was gone now.

"You don't waste any time, do you?" he said. "But no. No problems."

"Okay. Let's say that, then."

What did she mean by that? How much did she really know?

"I have an open position in Marketing. We need a new head of analytics. Interested?"

The analytics head was a prestigious job in many people's eyes. He was a little surprised she'd offer it to him at this point. He hadn't exactly been minding his career lately.

"I don't know...," he said, a little surprised by the offer. He didn't have time to finish the sentence.

"Think about it," Layla said. She got up to leave but before she did Hugo could swear she caressed his leg with her foot. It was subtle, in such a way that you couldn't tell if it was deliberate or by accident.

She smiled and left with her half-eaten lunch for the disposal bin. Hugo sat for a while, unable to put together a single coherent thought.

"Where the hell did you go?" Hugo asked when he came back up.

"Sorry. I just had to leave. There's just something about her that I can't stand."

"You're in love with her, that's what it is."

"Ha!"

"It's true. You just can't see it. Mr. Pickup Artist."

"Okay. That has to be it, then. It's those damn fish-nets that does it."

Bernie spat his Juicy Fruit with the precision of a marksman, hitting the trash can some ten feet away. He immediately folded in another one.

"What did you talk about after I'd left?"

"We bad-mouthed you, of course."

"How nice."

"But seriously, she offered me a job."

"Really?"

"Yes. They need a new analytics head."

Bernie smiled. "Is that something you might consider?"

Hugo hesitated, but said no.

"You keep focused on your goal now. Write the book. Nothing else."

He was right. The job sounded nice and secure but in the end it was really just more paper shuffling. The only thing separating that job from the one he had now was that there were other things printed on the papers. They still needed to be shuffled.

But part of him was definitely enticed by the idea of getting the ubiquitous T-Rexian surveillance machine off his back. Although, there was by no means any guarantee that it would be that much different with Layla. Hugo had accepted the fact that he didn't get along well with authority. Bosses were all power-hungry control freaks, horny for meddling with people's lives.

"I can understand if you're tempted," Bernie said. "Even if I like what you're doing now with the novel and I look forward to reading it, I realize that it must be a real strain on you to keep up the lies. A new job would reset everything. Turn everything back to normal."

"Safe and secure, huh?"

"Exactly."

But Hugo didn't want safe and secure. He wanted to scam the pants off the T-Rex. If he stopped writing the novel the T-Rex would win!

*Captain Ahab has to hunt his whale.*

He smiled at that analogy.

*That goes into the book! References to serious literature will make me look smart.*

Bernie tapped the table with his knuckles, as if he wanted extra attention. "But, hey... if you decide to take that road with Layla, be careful. She strikes me as very clever. Manipulative. She never plays with an open hand."

"Yeah. She seems pretty good at the whole office politics thing."

"Yes. And don't forget about the rumors."

"The sex rumors, you mean?"

"It's more than just some tardy behavior. She supposedly withheld a young male employee's bonus for refusing to go home with her after the Christmas party a few years ago. Before you started working here."

"Really? Sounds like baloney to me."

"Maybe."

"I mean, isn't it typical that rumors like that float around people like her? Women are not necessarily manipulative sluts just because they wear miniskirts."

"Yeeeeaaahh, maybe you're right. Just keep your

eyes open, kid."

Hugo guessed if anyone knew, it would be him. Bernie never bragged about his conquests but one thing was clear, he was above triple digits in his lifetime. His experience with women was unmatched.

That afternoon he couldn't write. Layla's offer was constantly on his mind, blocking his writing efforts. It surprised him that he couldn't let it go. It surprised him even more that he actually felt himself wanting the job. A part of him couldn't let go of the idea of being a good boy and climbing the corporate ladder.

After getting another cup of coffee he sat down and opened his word processor. Not necessarily to write, but to remind himself of what was important.

*It's nice to make money.*

Writers work for years without making a dime and when they finally get something published they get a pitiful little check and a few measly bucks in royalties, if you miraculously manage to sell out the advance. When you sold all the copies that you're going to sell you're not exactly rich. Unless your name is Stephen King.

During the same period of time he would've made many times that after tax, working at FastCredit. He had made huge amounts every year since he started here. Where the fuck had all that money gone? Not a penny saved. Everything had been put into their home. New kitchen, expensive furniture, luxury vacations. All of which felt pretty meaningless now.

So he couldn't just let Layla go. He decided to do some more checking. It couldn't hurt.

*Right?*

He knew very well that he couldn't let the process go

too far. Once you show interest it's very hard to, as Bernie says, get the shit back into the horse. He'd feel obliged to take it. He still decided to talk to Layla later that afternoon.


Besides the usual interior decorating with sterile office furniture in fake pine, computers, printers, fireproof file cabinets, Layla's office was decorated with drawings made by her children. The ones from her previous marriage. There were rumors floating around that the T-Rex wouldn't let her have pictures of them in their home since he wasn't their father. Apparently, Layla had spilled the beans about that at some drunken office party a few years ago.

Hugo made out the artwork to be of dogs, maybe cats, bicycles, rainbows and family members. They were plastered all over the wall. All of them placed so that you couldn't help noticing them as soon as you entered through the door.

"This is my youngest," Layla said and pointed to a really ugly piece of work, probably meant to be a dog but which looked more like a centipede, or something. It had legs all over the place.

Hugo of course already knew way more than he wanted about her kids. It wasn't the first time they had talked and she, like most mothers, bragged about her averagely gifted little brats as soon as she got the chance.

She continued with telling him that she had three kids. The oldest one was in high school, the middle one just starting junior high and the youngest, a girl, was eight. It was this little girl who had drawn all the pictures.

"Aaahhh," Hugo said, trying his best to fake interest.

"Aren't kids adorable?"

"Yeah... sure."

"Isn't it time for you and your girlfriend soon? Get married? Have kids?"

That's something you get to hear on a daily basis as soon as you're past thirty and still childless. Hugo had learned to just shrug it off and change the subject as quickly as possible.

"The job," he said. "Tell me more about it."

"Straight shooter too! I knew we'd get along fine, the two of us."

Layla got up from her chair, walked around her desk and sat down on the edge. Her short skirt slid slightly up along her thighs and revealed the lace of her hold-ups. Hugo saw that she noticed but she made no attempt to conceal them. Instead she started rocking her leg back and forth, her foot pointed towards him, with the back of the shoe dangling off her heel.

"The job, yes," she said, and softly bit her lower lip. She looked him in the eyes and held her gaze, more like she wanted to rip his shirt off than as if she was trying to recruit him for a job. Hugo couldn't decide if he was amused or disgusted. Or, for that matter, aroused.

"Are you trying to seduce me, Mrs. Robinson?"

"What?"

He thought a bit of humor would lighten up the situation. But that's the thing with reference comedy. If you're unfamiliar with the reference you won't get the joke.

"A joke," he said.

"You're a little prankster, aren't you?" she said, and laughed. An obvious fake laugh.

That little piece of verbal exchange was then followed by a few awkward smiles before she finally starting talking about what he came for. The job. He didn't find out anything more than he already knew except that he shouldn't expect a raise if he took it. The finances didn't allow for it.

"Think about it," she said before he left her office. "I need a reply in a week or so."

"I will," Hugo said and left.


Wednesday. Hugo had forgotten it was afterwork time with the gang. He hadn't heard anything about it so he called Nicolas around four to see if it was still on. They decided to skip it. Nella was still sick. Benzo was busy jonesing for Xanax and with the IT project from hell.

Hugo seized the opportunity to tell Nicolas about the job offer. His reply wasn't surprising.

"Take it," Mr. Square advised. "You know I think what you're doing is insane."

Hugo offered up his usual objections and they went through all the arguments again. Nick was a hard case to crack. No arguments would take on him. He went head on into one of his long John Galt-like rants that never seemed to end. Of course, that was Galt-like as in relentlessly droning on forever and ever and ever and eeeeeeh-ever, repeating the same point over and over until the end of time. Not the libertarian discourse. Nick was painfully middle of the road liberal.

"If you want to write, something of which I personally can't see the point, but that's a different matter completely, maybe you do, and I guess others do too, then you'll have to write in your spare time, during the night, in the mornings, maybe even a paragraph or two at work if you don't have anything to do, I mean really don't have anything to do, that is..." And on it went. Without pauses. The man had a lung capacity of a whale.

Hugo drifted away in a haze of thoughts and only came back in at the end.

"...but I think you should take the job and stop with all that nonsense you're doing. It's dangerous, and morally ambiguous at best."

*Good thing then, I have very flexible morals.*

But he guessed Nick's square, inside the box, mechanical perspective on life had its uses. Hugo just didn't want to follow it. He didn't want to dump another novel project into the bottom of his drawer. It was already full of stuff collecting dust.

That night he told Jessica about the job offer as well. Her reaction was one of relief. Not one of genuine joy, like if you win the lottery, but rather as if she had been waiting for some life changing test results from the doctor.

*Congrats! You don't have cancer!*

All the stress was gone. When he told her she leaped into his arms.

"Really! I'm so happy for you."

When he told her he hadn't decided if he was going to take it her mood immediately went south. He could see the disappointment in her eyes.

*Oh wait! Looks like I missed a lump there. You do have*

*cancer!*

He tried to assure her he might still take it, but it didn't help. They spent another silent evening in front of the TV, watching one of her reality shows. Hugo was too tired to try to fix things. Or argue over what to watch.

**12**

It was time for one of the office world's most pointless elements. *The Personal Development Talk*. Hugo had forgotten all about it and wasn't prepared. Not that you had to be. It was, like most other things here, a pointless exercise in paper shoveling that was quickly forgotten by all involved as soon as it was over.

"I agree," Bernie said. The PDT was one of his many favorite subjects to dump on. "There's not much substance to those talks. You're just placed somewhere in that damned performance matrix, somewhere slightly below average if he's not satisfied with you and somewhere slightly above if he is. No matter how hard you work you'll never end up at the top. And no matter how crappy you are you'll never end up at the bottom. Nobody wants to risk getting into too much of a conflict, or hurting anyone's feelings by giving you a potentially insulting rating. It's all just another prime example of corporate bullshit."

It was all old news that they had discussed a thousand times before. Office conversations have a tendency to repeat themselves.

"So you haven't looked at the material?" Bernie continued.

"No. I'll glance at it five minutes before it's time. Unless the procedure has changed it won't be a problem."

"Just don't forget to give yourself a credible placement in the matrix and you'll be fine. Not too high up. There has to be room for...hmmmrf...*development*. And don't mention your salary despite that being the only question of any *real* importance. He'll just say that this isn't a salary negotiation and not the time for that discussion."

Hugo smiled. He had been through five or six of these talks during his career and Bernie's advice was really superfluous. Bernie himself had probably done more than ten or fifteen of them with all those years in the business. He was even around in those days before the *Personal Development Talk* even existed. He always said that those were better days when the business world wasn't all bullshit. Well, well. They exist now. No point in whining about it and just deal with them.

"Have you heard the rumors, by the way?" Bernie changed the subject. "About Frank?"

"No. What?"

"Apparently his vacation home burned down."

"Really!"

"I'm not sure if it's true. I've just heard the rumors."

Hugo didn't know what to believe. If it was true it could explain some of the T-Rex's odd behavior. The way he just flew off the handle for nothing. He was stressed out. Or maybe he was just an asshole.

Anyway, he had to go prepare for the talk now. He excused himself and left.

When it started, the T-Rex was already sitting in his chair. He had sort of a sunken down posture, slightly nonchalant, and started as usual with rubbing his hands together. What he meant to convey with these silly theatrics Hugo could only guess. He kept doing it for almost a minute before even opening his mouth. Hugo tried to stay cool before what he thought could only be another avalanche of criticism and illogical accusations.

Several times during this hour-long minute the T-Rex seemed to want to throw himself into some rant but he just fell silent again, leaning back into his nonchalant posture every time and continued with the rubbing hands thing.

*I wonder if he'll say anything about that burned down vacation home. Probably not.*

Hugo squirmed in his seat. He was both nervous and bored at the same time. He tried to squirm discreetly, but in his mind he tossed and turned wildly. Had he really tossed around like that he would have been thrown off the chair. He just wanted to get the hell out of there, back to his new reality, back to writing his book.

*Bored, that's a given. But why am I nervous? I'm not supposed to care about this stuff anymore. The only thing I should worry about is the novel and whether or not he's on to my little scheme.*

It didn't help telling himself that. No matter how confident you are, you're always nervous when someone is about to cast judgment on you.

When the T-Rex finally stopped rubbing his hands together (maybe they were starting to chafe?) and started talking, he opened with a compliment.

"You've handled the revision very well. I have gone through some of the material very thoroughly and you've done a good job. It's accessible and provides an easy overview."

That statement was confirmation that the T-Rex was either a complete idiot or a liar. Hugo's improvised re-dating scheme might fool someone just taking a quick glance but not anyone taking a deeper look. In fact, just looking a page for more than ten seconds would probably reveal everything as the pitiful scam it was.

*Everybody lies.*

Or maybe he underestimated just how little the T-Rex actually knew about things here.

*Can he really be that stupid?* Nobody *is that stupid.*

"Great!" Hugo said, playing along. "I'm glad you're happy."

The T-Rex didn't go into it any deeper and just changed the subject. Hugo took that as confirmation that he had gotten away with it. It didn't matter if the T-Rex was stupid or just a liar. The scam had worked. For now.

"I appreciate what you do but there are still things we need to discuss," he said. "Management still think your reports are not good enough. They're not happy."

There it was again. The reports.

"The quality," the T-Rex said and paused for a long time as if he was trying to give weight to what was coming next. It all seemed highly artificial, theatrical. "The quality... has dropped in the last few months."

*Yeaaa-ah! Since you got here, bitch!*

The T-Rex continued. "Apparently you missed the entire downturn in the economy. Management aren't happy with that. We never had the chance to adapt because of your miss."

*Idiot! ARRRRGGHHH!*

Exactly what he had pointed out all along. In those reports he had sent. The ones that came back with a thousand corrections.

"Do you have any explanation for this, Hugo?"

*I've heard of office back-stabbing but this is getting ridiculous.*

He had gone into this meeting with the intention of just nodding along and agreeing but now he was furious. It was one thing if the T-Rex was a little dissatisfied with his performance, he could live that down easily, but this was placing the entire downturn of the business on him. He was making him a patsy. If the rest of the management team were sold on that idea, he was finished. It didn't matter if he were to take Layla's offer or continue with the book or whatever.

He was thoroughly pissed off now, like a pressure cooker with bum fail safe, waiting to blow and spew the steamed broccoli all over the fucking kitchen. He just *had* to defend himself.

"Are you serious?" he said. And then the shit hit the fan again.

"What do you mean?" the T-Rex said.

"Pinning this on me?"

"Pinning what on you?"

"The reports!"

"Of course. They're yours."

"No, they're not anymore. They're yours! You change everything in them after I send them to you."

"This again? Why would I change your reports?"

"FUCK! It's like talking to a retard. Why don't you just admit to changing them? This is beyond ridiculous."

Hugo kept going. "I pointed out already eight months ago what was going to happen."

"Are you accusing me?" the T-Rex said, now all red faced again, jumping up and down in his chair.

"I'm not taking the fall for something you did."

"You are dangerously close to an official warning, Hugo. I have kept Bryce and HR up to date with your attitude problems, just so you know. This goes all the way to the top."

Unlike the other shouting matches they'd had, Hugo's nervousness had disappeared this time. He was full of confidence in this very moment. Maybe it was the adrenaline kick from anger. He just wasn't going to take crap like this, no matter the consequences.

"Fine," Hugo said. "Do what you have to do. I still have all the original reports before your changes. Maybe I'll show them to a few select people who might be interested? Huh? How 'bout that?"

The T-Rex fell silent again. It was another bluff. Sort of. He probably had some of them somewhere in his humongous inbox but he had no idea where. It wouldn't be easy to find them.

"Okay," the T-Rex said. "This is getting out of hand. You have to calm down so that we can talk about this like adults."

143

Well, Bernie had been right. He had definitely been sidestepped but he still marveled at the clumsiness of the T-Rex's strategy. So incredibly arrogant to just deny something so obvious and think you can get away with it just because you're the boss. Most of the time bosses do get away with things. The balance of power is always tipped in their favor, but this was just insane. Hugo didn't care about what agenda was behind all this anymore, whether it was the T-Rex's personal ambition or some larger conspiracy to clear management's name. Besides, whatever it was it would go into the book. It was a dynamite plot twist. He just had to survive to write it.

"Let's leave this," the T-Rex said after rubbing his fingertips for another half a minute or so. "We won't get any further with this. I'll will have to try to find a way to work with these reports that will suit both of us."

Hugo didn't mind moving on. He had calmed down a little and reminded himself that it was just good if order was restored. That way he could keep up the writing. They moved on to the performance matrix. Nothing too surprising there. He was placed just below average. Hugo just nodded and agreed. He was exhausted now after the outburst. The T-Rex didn't seem to have any fight left in him either. They finished up and Hugo went back to his cubicle. The T-Rex never mentioned anything about his vacation home.

After the talk Hugo took a walk down by the water. He needed to think, catch his breath. For the first time he actually felt as if he was in real trouble.

No matter what happened it would be difficult to finish the book now. If he was fired for negligence there wouldn't be any severance package. He would need a new job right away just to stay afloat. If he wasn't fired he would probably have to endure ever-increasing pressure from the T-Rex and maybe the rest of the management. That would make it difficult to keep up the scheme. Layla's offer was suddenly more attractive than ever. He should probably grab it now, get that fresh start before everything turned to shit. Only problem was... he didn't really want to.

When he got home that day Jessica was already back from work. He was kind of pissed off because he hadn't written anything the entire day. Jess had left work early and he found himself being disappointed that she was already home. He had looked forward to throwing his feet up on the Danish design coffee table and going to town on the remote. There could be no doubt that their relationship had cooled a lot lately.

Now they would probably just argue over his writing ambitions. When they sat down to eat he told her about the development talk, about how the T-Rex was pinning everything on him. He had hoped for some sympathy.

"Maybe it's *your* perspective on things that's troubling here," she said. "Maybe you should take a look at what *you're* doing."

Neither of them went into any details. They had done that many times by now. Hugo just had to conclude that he didn't have Jess on his side anymore.

Funny thing was, it didn't even make him sad. He still had feelings for her but they were flat somehow, like a stale beer. He had never experienced that before and didn't know what to make of it. He loved her but

145

there was no passion. He wanted her to be well but he didn't care about her. He wanted her to be around but he never missed her when she wasn't. He didn't feel guilty about what he had done. He probably never would.

**13**

The summer was coming to an end and that meant it
was time for the big annual company party. It was also
a *kick off*, another one of the financial services world's
many bullshit activities where everyone is fed baloney
to build *team spirit*.

Hugo had been so busy with all the writing and
scheming that he had forgotten to bring the proper *corporate function* attire. Suit and tie, that is. He would've
never made it home and back to Covent Garden, where
the atrocity would take place, so he had to make do with
what he had. It wasn't a complete disaster. He had a

standard white bank shirt on and the bottom half of a dark suit. Shoes were okay and he had his navy blue jacket. Only thing missing was the tie and he knew Bernie had a bunch of spares in his bottom drawer.

"Take this," Bernie said, holding a black tie up against the light, carefully inspecting it. "I only spilled red wine on this one. It won't show."

*Black pants, black tie, white shirt and a navy blue jacket! Jess would've killed me if she saw it.*

Hugo noticed that for the day the dark mood had been swept away. "Party oooooonnn. Whuuhuuuu!" The young girls in customer service were screaming and giggling while flitting about and getting ready. Someone had arranged for some shitty speakers which had been hooked up to a laptop, playing all those old Eighties hits that even God had forgotten all about.

"What's with the Eighties that is so enticing?" Bernie said. "I mean, whhhhhyyyyy Rick Astley, Taylor Dane and Bananarama? Can't they at least play some of the stuff that was actually good?"

"I didn't think you liked anything from the Eighties?" Hugo said. He knew Bernie was heavily into Seventies rock and its über pretentious cousin, symphonic rock. Asia, Yes, Genesis and other kinds of crap that most other people barfed on.

"Yeah, I do. Some Ultravox maybe, Talk Talk. Blondie. Early U2."

Those were all artists that Hugo liked as well. Maybe not Blondie. He preferred singers who could carry a tune.

"I'm sorry, guys," Benzo said. "If it's the Eighties, it's lame. It doesn't matter what it is."

"Uhmm, Iron Maiden?" Hugo said. Benzo wasn't wearing his usual Maiden shirt today, but that didn't mean it was all forgotten.

"Except Maiden. Of course." Benzo smiled.

"Blondie is at least partly late Seventies," Bernie said.

"Splitting hairs much?"

Bernie was a complex man. Hugo couldn't really see what Blondie and Ultravox had in common with Genesis and Yes. Bernie obviously could. With Genesis, Bernie of course didn't mean the easy listening elevator music of the Eighties when Phil Collins dominated the band, but the over pretentious Seventies stuff with all the endless drum solos and guitar masturbation.

In the men's room all the young boys stood tying their ties over and over again to get the knot and the length right. They splashed cologne over their chests like there was no tomorrow. Hugo guessed the equivalent things went on in the ladies' room. The stench of cheap hooker had spread well into the hallway outside.

The managers had set up a table with alcohol and snacks in the kitchen areas, a warm-up before those funky British taxis would take them all to the premises where the kick off would take place. The premiere of the new TV ad was the main event. It had cost a fortune and management had spent weeks building up expectations.

Hugo and Bernie had parked their asses on the kitchen sofa and started to knock back a few beers. It was a little too early in the afternoon to be okay but they didn't care.

The rest of the staff started falling in pretty soon anyway.

149

Girls have a hard time before big company things. They usually wore cocktail dresses, something you wouldn't wear at work (at least not at FastCred) so they had to bring the entire kit from home. Dress, make-up, high heeled shoes, the works. They spent most of the time after four getting ready.

It's easier for men. Social function and bank wear is practically the same thing. Suit and tie. Although the dress code at FastCredit was relaxed for British conditions, meaning some people sometimes left their tie at home.

Some of the younger guys wore make-up.

"I don't get that," Bernie said. Not surprising for an old-timer like him.

"You're too old to get it," Hugo said. He never wore make-up himself. Perhaps because he too was just barely too old to have jumped that particular train.

The fact that it was so much more complicated for the girls to get in their party outfits turned the beginning of the warm-up into a total sausage fest. Nella was the first of the girls to arrive. It didn't mean she took her preparations lightly. She was absolutely stunning in her heavy but classy make-up and black cocktail dress cut just above her knees.

"If you don't yak so much it's pretty quick," she said when one of the young guys (Luke was his name, if Hugo recalled) from customer service asked her why she was done so much faster than the others. Nella wasn't as chatty as the average girl. A straight shooter by comparison, she said what she really meant most of the time instead of wrapping up everything in subtle enigmas. A girl that preferred beer over white wine and liked sports.

*A lot of men's dream girl.*

She didn't take anyone's breath away on a normal day but would definitely turn some heads when dressed up like this.

As people fell in, the volume of both the music and chatter went up. Some of the girls even started dancing and skipped songs on the laptop to whatever they wanted to hear (still only Eighties stuff, of course).

Benzo finally showed up and sat down on the armrest of the sofa Bernie, Nella and Hugo occupied. By now all the proper seats were taken. The ones standing watched the sofa like hawks in case someone went to the bathroom or to refresh their drink. This late into the warm-up it was all a reversed game of musical chairs. Whoever got up lost. It was only fair and everybody knew it.

Benzo wore a jacket but no tie.

"I don't have one," he said. "I'm the IT guy. I don't do banking stuff so I don't need one."

"Maybe IT is something to go for then," Hugo said. He hated wearing ties.

Nobody mentioned Hugo's writing, an implicit contract between them all. When the business met like this he still did what he was supposed to do. Everyone played along.

Soon it was time to head for the party premises and the conversation turned to logistics. Who was driving? Who was still sober? Who had room in their car? Who was going to take a taxi? Some were taking the Underground, other argued the bus would be more comfortable, some was even going by bike, maybe to get out of having to split the cost for a cab. Or did the company pay? Nobody knew and the big cheese had already left to prepare.

"I'll get a cab for us four," Bernie said. "I'll pay and that's that. I'll try taking it as an expense later. If it clears it does, otherwise who cares."

"Yeah," Hugo said, "but take it easy. We don't wanna be early. I hate sitting around before everyone else gets there."

Logistics always works itself out despite all the booze and imperfect information involved.

Management had rented some kind of ballroom. Hugo had never been there before. It had two big rooms, one which held the dance floor where drunk girls would shake their hips seductively and drunk guys would do the white man dance until the wee hours of the morning. (Come to think of it, FastCredit was a white ass bank). All to more Eighties music of course, now through some lame cover band instead of low quality streaming. Most of the management team were born in the mid to the late Sixties so the Eighties was their decade as well.

Hugo and his entourage sat down on the edge of the stage, waiting for the dinner to start in the other room. You couldn't tell from this evening that FastCredit had gone through a crisis. Live music, three course dinner, open bar. Management had puked money all over this thing.

"They have to keep up the illusion that everything is all right," Bernie said. "To motivate the staff until the bitter end."

"Now you're being cynical," Nella said. "They can't get any credit from you, can they?"

One thing was for sure at least. Whatever happened tonight, whatever would be said, the booze was going to pour.

"Open bar and banking people," Benzo said. "A recipe for disaster."

"The Brits are the fattest, most alcoholic people in all of Europe," Bernie said. "Almost up to US standards. It'll be a blowout."

Hugo smiled. He doubted Bernie could prove that. Fattest, probably, but the drinking? What about the Swedes, the Fins, the Poles and the others in the Vodka Belt?

Bernie went to the bar to order a drink. Hugo went with him.

"A Perseverance Drink!" Hugo said after the bartender gave him his gin and tonic.

"That's right! Bernie said and raised his glass. They toasted and took a sip. "The best drink there is!"

Bryce finally showed, half an hour late. He had Layla beside him. A good thing, Hugo guessed, because her shrill voice was probably the only thing that could quiet the already drunk staff. Hugo covered his ears when he saw her prepare her shout.

"QUIET!"

*In space no one can hear you scream. Unless you're Layla.*

After another minute of hushing and urges for the staff to settle down Bryce could finally announce the party started.

Free placement, to everyone's relief. That way you don't risk ending up next to someone you don't know! Or someone you don't like. Hugo and the entourage sat

153

together.

The starter was already served, waiting on the table in neat rows. The napkins were folded and there was cutlery for all three courses as well as three different wine glasses. The first one was already filled with a red wine.

The starter appeared to be some sort pâté.

"Shit," Bernie said.

"What?" Nella said. "Don't like pâté?"

"No, I like it. I just mean it looks like shit. It literally looks like the stuff I squeezed out this morning."

"Awhh! Gross!"

"It's more neatly shaped, though."

"This is completely wasted on my primitive palate," Hugo said. "I'm not nearly cultivated enough to eat pâté."

"Stop complaining!"

Benzo didn't say anything. He just poked at it a little with his fork. Bernie started eating.

"They haven't said we could start," Nella said.

"I don't give a shit."

"I thought you didn't like it?"

"Didn't say that. Said it *looked* like shit. It tastes good."

Hugo laughed. Rude, but refreshing somehow.

When Bryce had stopped talking and said everyone could dig in, Bernie was finished. He chugged down the wine and went back to sipping on his Perseverance Drink, which he still hadn't finished.

After the starter the kick off was launched. Bryce went up on the smaller stage in the corner to the music of Snap's Nineties hit *I Got the Power*. He always did that on occasions like this, and just like always it drew both enthusiastic applause and laughs.

Bernie and Hugo looked at each other and shook their heads. It would've been funny if someone else had thought of the idea to walk on to that song. That wasn't the case. Bryce had chosen it himself, which of course just made it pathetic.

Bryce started talking. He lingered a long time on last year's and this year's first quarter results. Not surprisingly, that was the time when things still were okay. He breezed past the downturn as if it was of no importance whatsoever. But at least he mentioned it. Hugo thought that was a small step forward.

The rest of the speech was a results comparison with their competitors and how superior they had been, during the good times, of course. He finished with some generic pep talk about how FastCredit was facing the future with *guns loaded*, with *team spirit* and *blah, blah, blah*. Hugo stopped listening.

Bryce turned it over to Layla, who started talking about the future marketing strategy. She made a huge spiel about FastCredit becoming a *serious* bank, more akin to the majors like Barclays, Chase, Bank of America and Citibank, a strategy that would separate them from the not so serious banks that were their current competitors.

"Is it just me," Hugo said, "or does this rhyme badly with what Bryce just said?"

"Mmm," Bernie said and paraphrased Shakespeare. "To lend or not to lend? That is the question."

Nobody laughed.

Then Layla rolled out a big screen TV and ran the

commercial that would bombard viewers across the UK. In it, an orangutan came into a bank wanting to loan money. An advisor approved the loan immediately and then FastCredit's logo was plastered all over the screen with the catch phrase 'so simple even a monkey can do it!'

"Serious bank, huh?" Bernie said and laughed a little too loud.

After the talking was done the entree was served, slightly late. By now Hugo was suffering from severe hunger pangs since he had deliberately starved himself all day for this very occasion. They served warm roast beef, on a bed of fresh greens and potatoes.

"Finally," Bernie said. "Some meat!"

"Pâté is meat too," Nella said.

"Shut up! You know what I mean."

Hugo was mostly quiet throughout dinner. He just chewed away at the tender meat. The red wine kept pouring and Bernie did his tired old joke pretending to be a wine connoisseur, tasting it and concluding, "I believe it's red!" They others at the table did their best to squeeze out a courtesy laugh.

The dinner went on for an hour and a half. There were no more speeches or kick-off related tidbits. The wine was quickly and efficiently refilled as soon as the glass approached empty, so when Bryce finally got up to inform them all that there would soon be dancing in the other room everyone was more than a little drunk. Bryce himself seemed to have obvious trouble with his sense of balance.

"Whoa! I've sat down for too long," he said.

"Yup, the sitting is the problem," someone shouted,

and was rewarded with laughs and applause. Hugo didn't catch who said it.

After dessert and coffee (served with *liquor* on the side, of course) everyone moved in to the dance floor. Most went straight for the bar, others parked their asses right down by the tables in the corners. The band opened with Bon Jovi's *Living on a Prayer* and just kept the Eighties hits rain in after that. Hugo could identify a few Nineties songs as well, although no grunge or anything even resembling an aggressively distorted guitar.

A group of girls started dancing with each other and sang along with all their might. Thankfully the music was so loud you could barely hear their undoubtedly off-key wailing.

After a while they started to pull reluctant guys up on the floor.

"I never dance when I'm sober," Hugo said.

"You're still sober?" Nella said.

"Ish!" He had no intention of reaching such a level of inebriation that he felt like dancing, but experience told him that would happen sooner or later anyway.

He, Bernie and Nella made their way to the bar. They each ordered a Black Label. While enjoying it Bernie and Benzo spewed out various put downs about their colleagues' dance styles. Some were funny and Hugo had to admit he was tempted to chime in, but he and Nella kept quiet. Hugo knew he was no better himself. Lower lip biting, off beat, white man dancing was all he knew. Nella could dance, though, but she wasn't the kind of person who would put people down.

"The girls are very pretty tonight," Benzo said.

Bernie put his hand on his shoulder. "Why don't you

go for it?"

"Nah. I don't know. I'm not good with girls."

"It's easy once you learn how to push their buttons."

"Why don't *you* make a move?" Hugo said, looking at Bernie. "You're supposed to be some kind of a pick-up artist, after all."

Bernie laughed. "Never at work. Never with girls you know and have to see the day after."

Nella looked pissed off. "So you're one of those ass-holes who prey on innocent girls and then don't call them afterwards?"

"Bernie McQueen at your service." He held out his hand for Nella to shake. She flipped him off.

*McQueen. How could anyone have such a cool last name combined with such a goofy first name? What were his parent thinking?*

"Seriously," he continued. "I'm not forcing anyone. They're not doing anything with me they don't wanna do. In my opinion, it's a misconception that women don't want casual sex."

He turned to Benzo again. "I'll tell you a strategy that will let you go from talking to kissing in just a few minutes. Try this. Go over to the one you like. Comment on something she's wearing as an opener, but no flattery or compliments on her looks. Then transition to some cocky-funny banter. Tease her about something. 'Wow, those heels are really high. Better watch out for low-flying air traffic with those on'. Haha! That kind of stuff. Call her by her name, talk to her like you already know her well. Touch her. Not on any of her naughty parts, but her shoulder, her lower arm, her elbow. Maintain a fairly intense eye contact, but not too much.

You don't wanna freak her out.

"Then after her bitch shield is down, stand reasonably close to her, not too close but definitely inside her personal space and say this: 'Oh, I just realized there's a girl in my personal space. Now I'm all nervous and shit.' Say it tongue-in-cheek, like it's a joke. This usually gets you a giggle. Ask her: 'What? Aren't *you* nervous?' Challenge her. If she says 'no', take a step closer, intensify your eye contact, but still tongue-in-cheek. You are now very close to her. Say: 'How about now?' If she still says 'no', you say, with a smile: 'Really? Let me know when you get nervous then.' Move in for the kiss. Very slowly. Most of the time she'll let you go all the way. Works seven times out of ten."

Hugo laughed. "You have actual statistics, haven't you?"

"Of course. I have a spreadsheet and everything."

"You're so full of shit!" Nella said. "No girl would fall for that."

"Reality says otherwise. Of course it helps if you look good. The better you look the less likely it is that she'll back away. But looks are not of any critical importance as long as you display attractive personality traits."

"Prove it," Nella said.

"No."

"Why not?"

Bernie smiled. "I don't feel any particular need for your approval. Besides, I told you, never with someone you know. But that's *my* criterion. Benzo here might feel differently, though?"

Benzo shook his head. "I could never do that. I

would just screw it up. Maybe even pee my pants."

"Come on, Benzo," Nella said and pulled him up on the dance floor. Bernie went off to take a leak. Hugo was alone at the bar. The T-Rex approached, probably to order another drink. He didn't seem to notice Hugo at first. When he did he got chatty. He was quite obviously drunk. Hugo prepared for the worst but the T-Rex was just super friendly. The personal development talk, the accusations, everything seemed forgotten.

"We've had our differences but it's only professional," he said. "Business, you know. I think you're a swell guy and if we had met outside of work for a pint or something we'd get along just fine."

"Of course," Hugo said. "I have nothing against you personally."

A lie, of course. You always say that when you're in conflict with one of your co-workers. He was sure the T-Rex lied just as much as he did.

The T-Rex kept on babbling but Hugo could barely hear him over the loud music. He too was becoming quite hammered and it was getting harder to concentrate. He got a pat on the shoulder and a "see you Monday" and then the T-Rex left. He decided to take a leak.

The corridor which housed the bathrooms also led out to a backyard. After he emptied his bladder he decided to get a breath of fresh air. There in the yard he saw one of the girls from the front end and Bryce clutching each other. Bryce had her pushed up against the wall and his hand was reaching in under her skirt. It was the sloppiest make out session he had ever seen.

"Confirmed once again," Bernie said, who had approached silently behind him. "Bryce is an ass."

"I can see that. This is disgusting. I think I just threw up a little in my mouth."

"They both have families, right?"

Bernie nodded. "Yup. Real class act, both of them."

"Would you have expected anything less?"

They went back inside.

"A few years ago," Bernie said, "Bryce had an affair with another one of the young front office girls. It ended badly, she quit. Now I don't mind a little office hanky panky if it's on equal terms, it's just not *my* thing, but he clearly used that girl to get his rocks off, all the while implying that there could be more between them. When she wanted him to make good on that he dumped her."

Nothing surprised Hugo about Bryce. He was a douche. They went back to the bar.

A few minutes later Bryce had retracted his tongue from the girl's throat and was eating a hot dog with Danni, a heavyset thirty-something girl from Marketing, and a couple of other girls. They were talking. Bryce of course wasn't interested in Danni. She was fat. One of the other, skinny, attractive girls — Anne, Hugo thought her name was — started pulling Bryce up on the dance floor. Bryce pointed to his hot dog and gestured that he hadn't finished yet. The girl didn't give up. She pulled and pulled until Bryce caved. He shoved the hot dog down between Danni's tits.

"Hold this, will you?"

Hugo and Bernie just stood there, jaws dropped. But Danni seemed to take it all very well. She just fished the dog out of her cleavage and ate it.

Hugo decided to rinse that last image away with another Perseverance Drink and another breath of fresh

161

air. This time he decided to go out through the main entrance. There was nobody there. Nice. A moment to himself.

He noticed a woman waiting by a car across the street. A fancy car. Looked like an Audi. One of the upper range models. So was the woman. Blonde, slim, skirt with the hemline just above the knees, very high heels. She was looking at him. A little more intensely than he was comfortable with. He was a little dizzy from all the booze and couldn't see who she was. He walked towards her and when he came closer he saw that it was Layla.

She waved.

*Do I walk over? Could be a bad idea? Party, alcohol, inhibitions a bit muffled. It would definitely be a bad idea. Screw it! Bad ideas are what make life worth living.*

"Mrs. Rex," Hugo said. "You look lovely this evening."

"Don't call me that."

"Yes. What is your last name, by the way?"

That intense eye contact was there again. She had her hands on her hips, she smiled. She bit her lower lip.

"Really? That's what you want to know right now?"

Hugo smiled. "I guess it can wait 'til Monday."

"That's better. You're looking handsome today, Hugo. Minus the hideous color mismatch, of course."

He smiled, tried to maintain that eye contact.

"I have my reasons for wearing this god-awful thing," he said. "I promise you I have better fashion sense than that."

"What reasons would those be?"

"I don't think I can tell you."

She took a step closer. She was now standing very close. He could smell her perfume. No alcohol on her breath.

*I guess she's tonight's designated driver.*

"A secretive fellow, are we?"

*Always keep your cool with women, no matter what they do.* Bernie had told him that.

"Are you flirting with me, Mrs. Rex?" he said.

"What if I am? And don't call me that."

"This is dangerous territory."

"What's life without a little danger every now and then?"

She moved a little closer still. Kissing distance, almost.

"I like your tie," she said and stroked it along his chest all the way down to his pants.

"You have a thing for younger men?" Hugo said.

She moved closer, her lips almost touching his.

"Who hasn't?"

Their lips touched. Just slightly. It was incredibly arousing.

"You're making my penis feel funny," Hugo said.

She pulled away, but still smiling seductively.

"Another time," she said. "Frank will be here any minute. We're leaving."

"I guess I should go then?"

"Yes. See you."

"Indeed."

He backed up a few steps while maintaining eye contact. He gave her one last smile and then turned and went back inside. Inside the doors he met the T-Rex, coat and everything on, ready to leave.

"I think your wife is waiting outside," Hugo said.

The T-Rex nodded. "See you Monday," he repeated.

Well, inside Hugo had another drink. It turned out that was the one that pushed him over the limit. He pulled Nella up on the dance floor. And he danced.

**14**

When you get to the office the day after a big company thing the mood is always a bit tense. Most people have something to regret, or at least fear they do, after such a blowout. The anguish and shame spread like a thick fog over the cubicle landscape.

When Hugo strolled through the office to the coffee machine he noted that all the greetings he got were unusually low key, and everyone but a few had difficulties maintaining eye contact.

Someone had groped, another one had said something they shouldn't, a third had hurled publicly. Hugo had danced, which was embarrassing for him. He had had the drunken *best buddies* talk with the T-Rex on top of that. Not to mention he had been felt up by his wife.

When he said hi to him this morning there had been tension. The T-Rex probably hadn't been drunk enough to have lost their little convo in the weekend's hangover haze. The T-Rex himself hadn't been in until eleven so he hadn't had a chance to notice Hugo's own late arrival. But it was business as usual again. The T-Rex didn't trust Hugo and he didn't trust him back.

He drifted lazily around the office to see if anyone was up for a chit-chat. And to test his shame and anguish theory. Front or back-office, it didn't matter. Everyone did their outmost to end the conversation as quickly as possible.

He ended up with Bernie as usual.

"What's up?" Bernie asked.

Hugo told him about the tension he experienced. Bernie didn't seem to care. "I don't feel anything like that anymore," he said. "What's the point? Tomorrow it will have eased up a bit. The next day some more, and come Wednesday it'll all be back to normal."

"You're untouchable, Bernie."

"You build up tolerance against that shit the longer you work in the business." He got up. "Come along, kid. I need caffeine." He took his cup with a few years' worth of burnt in coffee residue all over the inside but which he still never cleaned or even put in the dishwasher. "The grime adds flavor," he claimed.

"It's like a virus," he continued. "The tension thing, you know. Once you've had the flu a few times you build up a defense against it. When it comes around again it's milder. The next time milder still, and finally you're not hit at all."

Hugo seriously doubted that was how flu viruses worked, but he understood what he meant.

They chatted for a while. Afterwards Hugo went back to his cubicle. The navy blue jacket hung over the back rest, the screen saver rolled screenshots of his spreadsheets, the music from the internet radio played. Today he had brought one of his half-eaten stinky-lunches—mac'n'cheese drowned in Roquefort. The desk was a mess with *important papers*, books loaded with Post-its between the pages, binders, notes and printed emails.

All the tricks were in play and he couldn't help but feeling proud of what he had accomplished. He had written a third of the novel now and most of it on company time. It made him feel warm all over knowing he had wasted months of FastCredit's money on doing this.

He tried writing. Maybe it was a dull day. Maybe it was the echo of Layla's offer but he definitely had a case of writer's block. So much so that he even considered doing some *real* work! To put together a few binders for the revision.

*NO! It hasn't gone that far yet.*

After a few minutes of mentally whipping himself he got started, and had built up an impressive flow when the T-Rex showed up by his cubicle. By now he had built up a solid routine and simply Alt-Tabbed to a spreadsheet he kept open in the background. The T-Rex never suspected a thing.

"See you in my office," the T-Rex said. "We have some things to discuss."

He didn't seem to be in his usual pissy mood for once.

"We're getting a visitor," he said when they had sat down. "By a... Ab... Abhi... Abihman... Abhimanyu Hiran...Hiranyag...Hiranyagrbha." He stared at the paper, eyebrows raised. "Yes. That's probably how you

167

pronounce it. He's from the Head Office in New York. An Indian fellow."

FastCredit's middle levels overseas employed hundreds of people from India. Some of their names were real tongue twisters. Rex sounded like a retard trying to pronounce it, and Hugo had to work hard to suppress a real thigh-slapping belly laugh.

The T-Rex noticed his effort.

"Something funny?"

"No," he managed.

The T-Rex looked at him suspiciously. "He's here to observe our operation," the T-Rex continued. "I want you to take care of him while he's here. Show him around, make sure he gets lunch and so on."

"How long will he be staying?"

"Two days. Thursday and Friday next week. On Thursday he'll be in Corporate and on Friday here with us."

"Okay. Sure. I'll babysit."

"Another thing," The T-Rex said. "I'll be at Corporate three days a week from now on. I have been given the assignment to implement a new risk plan for them. Corporate has been a small operation up until now and they've been exempt from having one. But they're growing so I'll be their risk head too."

"Okay," Hugo said. "Sounds exciting."

*That would've been my job, asshole. If things were as they should be, that is.*

He wanted to say something but instead wished the T-Rex good luck and made a remark that it would be too bad they wouldn't see each other that much anymore. But of course this was awesome news. He would be able to write with far less disruptions now.

"That's not all," the T-Rex continued. "I'll be away the other two days as well for a while to come."

"Really?"

Could this really be?

"As you may have heard," the T-Rex said, with a bit of a distressed tone of voice, "my vacation home has burned down and I have a lot of trouble with my insurance company. Tons of paperwork, applications, affidavits, police reports, meetings this and meetings that. You have no idea how many problems I have. It's been going on for months now and it's killing me."

So it was true. He couldn't help it but he was almost overwhelmed with feelings of *joy*.

*Schadenfreude. Hehe. Germans. Leave it to them to come up with the word for malicious joy.*

"No, I haven't heard," he lied.

"So you'll be on your own for a while. Report directly to Bryce from now on."

Hugo left the T-Rex's office with a wide smile on his lips. He could finally breathe. At least for a while. He would use the time to write his ass off. But, he remembered, he also needed to talk to Layla about the job offer. He could still take it.


Later that day he was called into Bryce's office. It was actually the first time the two of them had talked for more than a few minutes, and talked about real things, not just idle small talk. Hugo had concluded that Bryce never fraternized with the little guy but Bernie had corrected him.

"He does, but only with people way down on the ladder," he explained. "People in Customer Services and Collections hang out with him from time to time. He only talks to people who're not too close to him career-wise. You know, people without enough inside knowledge to maybe question him, to challenge his leadership."

Maybe Bernie was right. Hugo often perceived Bryce as being on the defensive when you talked to him, even in more social situations.

Bryce would ask him what he was doing. Hugo had thought a lot about that particular question and what his reply should be. The trick was of course to say something that would make Bryce leave him alone. Since he didn't have any real work to do anymore except the audit and pumping reports full of raw data, he had to make something up. He preferably wanted to avoid the mess with the reports the T-Rex had usurped. Bryce might want to see them and Hugo had no control over the content anymore, despite them bearing his name.

He had to think of something and when cheating is on the agenda you go to the expert. You go to Bernie.

"Start an initiative," he said. "A project. Something that sounds complicated, important and beneficial to the firm but which is fuzzy and has no measurable out-come."

"Like what?"

"Okay, listen. FastCredit is a huge behemoth of an organization. There's no direct hierarchy. You report locally to the T-Rex, but also directly to New York, two units that otherwise have little to do with each other, right? They all in turn report to other units who report to other units who report to others still. They then re-port to senior management again in New York. On top all this there's a whole bunch of feedback channels to controllers and to the units who initially filed the report. It's all a maze of shit and nobody really has any over-view."

Hugo's head was already spinning. "Sounds like something I should be able to take advantage of."

"Exactly. Tell them you want to streamline the re-porting chain." Bernie paused for effect. "Tell Bryce there are so many reporting lines that you send the same, or nearly the same, reports multiple times to dif-ferent units and that it would be more efficient if you could simplify this. Use big corporate bullshit words like *finding synergies* and being *proactive* and shit. You know the drill. Emphasize that it could save the firm money by simplifying the bureaucracy. He'll buy it."

"But in reality I'm not doing anything, as usual?"

"Exactly. Nothing at all! And nobody will check up on you because they're not familiar with the problem. A problem you have partially invented yourself, but still, no one will have the energy to get involved. At the same time it will sound like you're going the extra mile which will give you serious cred with the big kahunas."

Hugo nodded.

*Impressive. Most impressive. Bernie is the King!*

"And should someone actually get nosey," he fin-ished, "you just say that the people involved at the re-gional and international levels were reluctant to change anything. Nobody will doubt that's true. It's what we in the business call a *win-win*."

Hugo took Bernie up on the advice and told Bryce

171

exactly what they had discussed. Bernie was right. It slipped right through. No hitch.

At three Hugo took a coffee break with Benzo in conference room one, which nowadays mostly resembled an IT chop-shop. Benzo was working on a broken machine. As far as Hugo could gather it was still that encryption software that was causing the problems. The support from regional IT had left a long time ago. They had given Benzo a week's worth of help and that was apparently sufficient in their eyes whether the problem was solved or not. Things were better, but not exactly *good*.

"The encryption software isn't communicating with the server," Benzo said. Hugo knew enough about computers to fix most common user problems himself (by restarting the machine—if that doesn't help it seems like little else will).

Benzo's eyes were bloodshot and had been so for about two weeks' time.

"I'm popping my Xanax like candy," he said. He really looked to be on the edge. "Time for a change of strategy." He got up from the chair.

"To what?"

"The technical term is *percussive maintenance*."

He went to the storage locker and came back with a hammer, a regular hammer the reception staff used to hang new paintings and such. He went to town on the machine with a psychotic fury that would put the T-Rex's spit-splashing rages to shame. And he was heavily dosed with Xanax at that! The machine bounced from the force of every stroke, the metal casing denting heavily. After about ten strikes Benzo stopped, exhausted. The screen went blank and that was the end of that computer.

"I need a vacation," he said, now smiling widely. "I'll just dump this piece of crap in the dumpster out back."

Nobody would miss it. Benzo was the one holding the IT inventory. He wouldn't have any problems cooking the books.

The noise had attracted a few curious co-workers. Hugo stepped out of the conference room to diffuse the potentially troublesome situation. "Everything is under control. Nothing to see here." He closed the door quickly before anyone had time to ask any questions. Benzo didn't need that type of attention.


At precisely two that day FastCredit got a visit from two gentlemen in dark navy blue suits. They had been flown in from New York, apparently. They were both hauling compact Samsonite wheelie bags.

"Chainsaw consultants," Bernie said. "Time to rationalize our staffing needs. Which of course is code for mass sackings."

"Don't jump to conclusions," Nella said, a little pissy.

"Hundred pounds I'm right?"

Pat Denham, FastCredit's HR manager, greeted them. "Another indication that I'm right," Bernie said. "Why else the HR manager?"

Bryce and Fred Barnes, another American brought in as the new Customer Services head also joined in. They closed the door and pulled the blinds.

Hugo couldn't recall getting an announcement about

any visitors. It was customary for management to send out instructions to everyone to dress appropriately before visits (meaning *wear your tie*). No announcement probably meant that Bernie was right. Management wanted to keep everyone in the dark as long as they could.

"Okay, let's assume you're right," Hugo said. "What does it mean for us?"

"Reviews. If they find that FastCred can do without you you're done."

Nella looked at Hugo. "Did you get caught or something?"

She said it with a smile but Hugo could sense the seriousness in her voice. He didn't have the chance to reply before Bernie cut in.

"No, no. Then Hugo would've been asked to join in. And besides, a whole host of warnings and reassignments and talks with staff shrinks and other such shit would have to take place before you sack anyone for not doing their job. It's policy. He's safe for now. No, this is about mass terminations. Or outsourcing. Or both. The two often overlap."

"So now it begins," Hugo said.

"Yup. It's on," Bernie replied.

Nella said nothing.


When Hugo returned to his cubicle he found an invitation to attend a conference in Paris. It had been forwarded by the T-Rex who explained he didn't have the time to attend himself because of the problems with his vacation home. He wanted Hugo to attend in his place.

The conference was mainly about some new reporting software.

The conference would be held on Wednesday next week and would entail a stay at the Warwick, right by the *Champs-Elysées*. He would be home again just in time to babysit Abhi...Abhiman...the Indian guy.

Hugo didn't mind, of course. A trip to Paris wasn't bad. He would probably not have time to do anything else but attend the conference but he would at least get to stay at a five star hotel and eat a luxury dinner in their restaurant. At FastCredit's expense.

Before the shit hit the fan here he had been to a few different conferences every year, but since the numbers went red most such activities had been deemed as *unnecessary excesses* by the New York office. Just as well. Most such gatherings were pretty pointless and could've been handled with web conference or even with a few phone calls. But business travel is a highly appreciated part of the financial services sector. It makes people feel needed and special to be sent on business trips.

*Yeah, you know what? I can't make your pointless little dinner party. I have an important business meeting to attend in wherever. I have to be at the airport early. You see, I'm much more important than you. That's why my company spends a lot of money sending me places. Do you travel in your work? You don't? Hehe... Of course you don't. You're just a pathetic loser, aren't you?*

He looked at the attendance list and saw that Gary, FastCred's relatively new CFO, was also invited. With any luck he could get him to delegate the trip to one of his people.

*Maybe I can get Nella to come along?*

175

Hugo went and checked with him. It turned out he wasn't sending anyone. The system in question had nothing to do with them.

"But they put you on the list for a reason, didn't they?" Hugo said. "Maybe send one of your staff? Everything is paid for anyway."

Gary bought it and agreed when Hugo suggested Nella.

"Thanks, Hugs!" Nella said when Hugo told her the news. "That was a pleasant surprise." She gave him a peck on the cheek. "It'll be tight with time, though. It's already next week."

"It'll be fun. We'll eat dinner together afterwards. The most expensive shit they have. And FastCred picks up the bill!"

"And afterwards we can hit a club!"

"Yeah! A nice change from shuffling papers. Just what the doc ordered."

Hugo went back and answered the invitation. He reserved two rooms.


It was Wednesday again. Both Nick and Nella could leave early for once so this time they didn't have to cancel.

"It's important to keep things like this going in times of crises," Nella said.

"So you've finally accepted that there is a crisis?" Hugo asked.

"Well...I suppose."

They ordered the usual—beer and chips, or *crisps* as the Brits call them. If you order chips here you get

*French Fries.* Weird. Lardy joined them for a while but made it clear he didn't have time to linger. Maya, his newly employed help, couldn't handle the bar alone yet.

"I'm not noticing any crisis," Lardy said. "Customers are flowing, like always. They drink just as much as always."

"Well," Nick started. He pulled on his little tousle on the top of his forehead and put on his worst professor face, the one he always had when he was about to lecture someone on some finer point of economic theory. "Firstly, bars aren't that much in the line of fire, so to speak. People want their liquor at the bottom of the business cycle just as much as at the top. Maybe even more during a crisis, to drown their sorrows. And secondly, the crisis probably hasn't spread beyond the banking sector yet. It's too early. It will, though."

"Is that so, professor Krugman?" Hugo said.

Lardy made a sound as if he was snoring. "Booooring."

Nicolas gave them the finger.

"So Hugo was right," Nella said.

"Bernie was right," Hugo corrected her. "He was the one who said we were heading into this shit storm."

"You said it would go to hell already when your old boss quit. I bow to your wisdom, Hugs. You were right."

"And now the chainsaw people have paid you a visit?" Nicolas said.

"Yup," Hugo said. "Layoffs are just around the corner."

"It doesn't have to be layoffs," Nicolas said.

"Exactly," Nella said.

"What the fuck? You just said I was right and now I'm not? What happened to bowing to my wisdom?"

"We might still make it, that's all."

"Not what Bernie thinks."

"Bernie this and Bernie that."

"He's been right about everything so far."

Nobody said anything.

"What do you think those people were here for then?" Hugo said.

"A new health care plan?" Nicolas said, and laughed loudly.

"I think you're all going to be sacked," Lardy said. "And then you'll all come here to drown your sorrows in my ale. Ker-Ching! Then you'll all find new jobs to hate and then that'll be that."

Hugo took a sip from his beer. "Maybe I'll start a bar? Out-compete you."

"Haha."

"I'm not kidding."

"You'd never be able to run a bar," Nick said. "You'd just drink all the beer yourself."

"And then you develop catastrophic liver failure and die," Lardy added.

"What is Jessica saying about all this?"

Hugo exhaled and stared down at his beer. He had avoided everything about Jess lately. He didn't talk about her, he didn't talk *with* her, he even tried hard not think about her. He had started writing more during the evenings, he went out jogging. All to avoid contact.

"I don't know," he said. "We haven't had much time to talk lately."

"What do you mean 'no time'?" Nicolas said. "You

live together."

"She has her job. I have mine. If you call mine a job. We're both busy."

He could see in their eyes they weren't buying it.

*Why would they, with such an awesome and well thought out lie? With all the accompanying facial expressions and body language and everything. I have to practice.*

Thankfully they didn't talk anymore about it. Instead they went over the bad times again, and the fear of losing their jobs. Hugo definitely didn't get the same resistance anymore when the crisis came up. As the evidence piled up it was only natural. Hugo resisted the temptation to say "I told you so!" What did it matter anyway?

He followed Nella to the bus before hitting the Underground. When only the two of them were together they seldom talked about the crisis. That particular bitching seemed to require a third party as a catalyst. Their alone time was always painless, caring and relaxed. They respected and knew each other so well they could let their differences slip through without conflict. Hugo felt it very liberating to have such a relationship with another person.

*Maybe that's why we've never done the girlfriend-boyfriend thing. Romance would probably ruin that.*

Despite that, there had always been that exquisite tension between them. On the physical level. But even that was mostly painless. Hugo had never regretted that night years ago, or what he had given up on by not pursuing a relationship. He was sure Nella didn't either.

They didn't say much on the way to the bus. It didn't matter. Even silence was comfortable with her. They split and Hugo headed for the Underground. He found a seat and dozed off, despite the massive crowding. It was a good nap. The best in a long time.

When he came home he told Jessica that he was going to Paris next week. He didn't mentioned that Nella was coming along.

**15**

Wednesday came. Hugo and Nella had shoved their carry-ons in the hatch above them and sunk into their seats. There was more air in the schedule than Hugo had first thought. The plan was to take off at eight and the conference didn't start until one, Paris time. Despite losing an hour there was no reason to get stressed out.

They landed at *de Gaulle* on time. FastCredit's environmental policy required them to take public transportation whenever they could. Taxis were a no-no unless it absolutely couldn't be avoided. FastCredit's way of giving back.

"Screw that!" Hugo said.

Nella looked at him with raised eyebrows.

"Oh yeah! That's just the kind of rebel I am."

They would still be reimbursed for a cab, something Hugo didn't get. If they really wanted to create incentives for people to use public transportation why not stop paying for taxis?

The conference took place in some office building in *La Defence*. Hugo and Nella sat in the back of the huge auditorium. Hugo half slept through the slides with images of the new software. He drifted off into thoughts about his novel, about Jess, about the T-Rex.

At half time they met Katja, a colleague Hugo had had quite a lot of interaction with over the years before the crisis hit. She was a Ukrainian girl with a thick Eastern European accent. She also worked in Risk. He had met her several times on conferences just like this one. She was strikingly beautiful, petite with dark hair and what he imagined typical facial features of Slavic women. High cheekbones, petite nose, the works. Hugo had always had a thing for Eastern European girls. There was just something about them that sent blood streaming towards his crotch area.

Hugo always flirted with her. It was fairly innocent, the way colleagues sometimes do. She flirted back. It was risk free, Hugo had always thought, since she worked in Paris and he in London.

She was a party girl and she suggested that the three of them do something later in the evening after the conference was over. She'd heard of a new club in some back alley behind Champs-Elysées that was supposed to be good.

"Great!" Nella said. "Awesome."

Hugo wasn't that excited. He had never really been that much into the whole nightclub scene but of course he would tag along. He wasn't in Paris every day. Some nightlife would probably do him good. Maybe the thump of the music would smash some of those annoying thoughts tumbling around inside his head.

When the conference was over he realized he didn't remember a thing that gray-haired square on the stage had said. He didn't care. If the T-Rex wanted an update he would just give him the booklet. Everything was very neatly summarized in it. So well, in fact, that there really wasn't any point in flying people in for a conference.

He and Nella ate dinner at the hotel. They ordered the full luxury menu, including starters, wine, dessert and cocktails afterwards. Katja joined them after dinner. They sat in the lobby bar and drank before taking off for the club. They ordered drink after drink, all going on FastCredit's account. They chit-chatted. Mostly about the crisis, of course. It wasn't just the UK branch that was failing. It might even have been worse here in Paris.

Once again ignoring the FastCredit environmental policy, they took a cab to the club. Hugo danced again. Kajta flirted with him all night. He flirted back. It was subtle, or at least so Hugo thought. Eye contact, caressing shoulders and lower backs. Nella saw what was going on, he was sure of it. At about midnight Nella said she was tired and wanted to go back to the hotel and sleep.

"Early flight tomorrow," she said.

Katja came back with them and when they arrived Nella said bye and went up to her room. He wasn't sure if she was pissed off or if she did him a favor by refraining from cock-blocking him.

"Let's go to your room," Katja said. Hugo didn't say anything about Jessica and Katja didn't ask. She knew they were together.

"Yes, let's," he said.

When they reached the room she threw herself on the bed and dragged Hugo with her.

"Kiss me."

He did. They took off their clothes. He had held back on the alcohol the last few hours at the club, just in case he would find himself in this very situation. He wasn't good on alcohol.

He had slept with nine girls in his life, he just realized. Katja would make it double digits. Not much to brag about in the locker room but still, a fully respectable number.

*It may be a bit silly, but these things are important to guys. Any guy who says otherwise is lying. It's hardcoded into us by evolution.*

He had learned from these nine girls he had before that satisfying a woman meant performing cunnilingus. That and a few fingers, maybe a pinky up her ass, would usually do the trick. Overwhelming stimulation on multiple strategic parts of the body. That's what got girls off.

Her pussy smelled and tasted like pussy. Something Hugo appreciated. He didn't like when it smelled like shower cream or lotion. After she came he quickly put on a condom and went inside her. He humped away with a fiery, lumbar-spraining, disc-slipping fervency. She came again. At least he thought she did. Might just have been cramps.

Sometimes he would lift Jess up after the second one and have her squat on him, both of them in a seated position. He would force her hips to rock back and forth hard and she would come a third time. But Katja had had enough.

"Now your turn," she said. "Fuck me."

She raised her legs straight up, and back, her feet almost touching her ears.

"Oh! Flexible. I like it."

He fucked her, violently, watching his cock go in and out. She was tiny and he looked huge. It was awesome!

*The most painless way to get a bigger dick? Get a small girl.*

"When you come," she said. "Pull off condom and come in face."

Jess had never let him do that. None of the others he had fucked either. "You sure? I didn't think girls really liked that."

"Some of us do."

"Really?" he said between his heavy breaths. "I have a huge load. Like, Peter North kind of huge."

"Who is that?"

"Google him. Now shut up! I'm about to google *you* in face."

Her accent was incredibly sexy. It drove him crazy. He couldn't hold back anymore and he did what he was told. She seemed to really enjoy it. He had saved up for quite some time and his load was white and thick. It covered her face, mouth, neck and breasts.

*Juuuust like in the pornos.*

Afterwards she put her arm around his neck and pulled him in and kissed him. She tried to push his cum back into his mouth. He tried to break free but she was surprisingly strong and he was weak after unloading. When he resisted she spat some in his face and pulled him in harder. The kiss seemed to last a long time, all the while he was trying not to taste his own jizz. When he finally broke free she spat some more in his face. She giggled. Hugo laughed as well. He wasn't upset, or disgusted. Just amazed. And maybe a little amused.

"What the FUCK, girl! Why?"

"So you remember me." She giggled. "How many girls do that to you?"

"Haha. None."

She was right. He certainly would remember her. His efforts to keep his mouth closed had only been partially successful. He had now tasted semen. His own, but still. He could never untaste it. But it was okay. It actually wasn't that bad. Salty. And something else that he couldn't quite identify.

*Maybe it's the pineapple?*

"Relax. Tasting yourself won't make you gay or anything."

He laughed again.

"I'm going to take shower," she said.

He fell back on the bed, exhausted. He didn't even care to wipe the cum off his face.


He showered after Katja was done. They lay naked in bed, her head resting on his chest. The room was spinning from the alcohol and exhaustion but it was okay. He didn't fall asleep like he always did with Jess. He wanted to enjoy the moment, take it all in. He felt her breath, her chest moving up and down gently against his side. Her breath smelled of alcohol, her hair of cigarette smoke. There was nothing about this that resembled Hollywood rom-com lovemaking. He loved it.

He knew he should feel guilty about cheating on Jess but he didn't. Instead he felt invigorated. *Reborn!* Well, almost. He still worked in a bank, but nothing was impossible in this moment, nothing was hopeless. He didn't have any feelings for Katja. Just raw animal attraction. It was the first time he had had this kind of relationship with a girl.

"You happy?" he asked.

"Yes. I come twice."

"Yeah, I know. Sorry. The booze made me a bit tired."

She giggled. "You are good. Eight out of ten."

"What the fuck? Just an eight?"

"Haha! Ok, nine out of ten. You are good with mouth. And you have good *pennis*." He laughed. It was the cutest mispronunciation of the word penis he had ever heard.

"You didn't fuck me from behind. I like."

"You never asked."

"And no ass play."

"Oh! You dirty girl. I'll step it up a bit the next time. So what was good then?"

"Yes. I show you how men have sex."

She got up and squatted by his feet. "Spread legs."

"What?"

"You are girl. I am boy."

She forced his legs apart and lay down on top of him, with her full weight over his chest. It was hard to breath. She started humping.

"This is a bit awkward." It was actually more amusing than awkward. He could barely keep himself from laughing. He wasn't sure if he should.

"Shut up!" she said and lay down even heavier on his chest. "You can breathe?"

"No, not really." She was really heavy despite being so petite.

187

"Exactly. This is how men have sex. They lay on you humping like spastic. They press chest so you can't breathe. Then they ask 'why you make no sound? You don't like?' I say 'I make no sound because you are smothering me, you bastard'."

He laughed. Sort of, at least, with almost no air left in his lungs. He could imagine what that was like with the weight of a full-sized man on top of you.

"They do this for few minutes," she continued. "Then come," she mimicked the sound of a man coming, "then roll off and fall asleep. Maybe little oral to top you off. If lucky!"

Hugo laughed. No wonder girls prefer to cuddle.

She rolled off him and kissed his cheek. "See you next time in Paris?"

"Yeah. Sure."

She got up and put her clothes on. She didn't want to spend the night. That was okay with him. No sentimental goodbyes, no fuzz. No guilt. She simply left and he fell asleep.

The next day he took Nella shopping. She didn't ask him what had happened last night. She barely spoke at all. Hugo didn't mind, but this time the silence felt a little uncomfortable. He had with him a list of things Jess wanted. Perfume, little jars of jam, chocolates and other things. The silence continued on the flight home. Hugo waited for the guilt to come. It never did.


Friday. Hugo was still a bit hungover from the trip to Paris. He felt dehydrated both from the alcohol and the sex.

*Two-day hangover? I didn't even drink all that much. I*

188

*must be getting old.*

He still didn't feel any regrets. He still hadn't told Jess. He probably wouldn't.

Time to get back to business. Writing, that is.

Lydia moved around her desk and sat on the edge of it. Her skirt slid up so I could see the lace of her hold-ups. She gave me a seductive look.

"I do believe you are trying to seduce me, Mrs. Robinson," I said.

"What?"

"It's a movie. *The Graduate? Dustin Hoffman? Anne Bancroft?*"

She seemed oblivious. The problem with reference humor is that it's not funny unless you are familiar with the source.

*How can you not have heard of The Graduate? I thought. She's as ignorant as she is hot.*

He stared at the paragraph. He liked writing about Layla, or Lydia as he called her in the novel. It was a perfect name. Similar to her real name and it was the name of Chinaski's first hook-up in *Women*.

The part with Layla/Lydia was fun and carefree, unlike much of the rest of it. Hugo's hero expressed doubt, the same doubt he had himself in real life. Was he doing the right thing abandoning his career? Because that was in fact what he was doing. There was no way he would be able to keep up the charade indefinitely. Today was the day Layla wanted her answer to the job offer.

He quickly Alt-Tabbed when she came by.

"How's it going, Hugo?" she said.

"Okay, I guess."

"Been thinking?"

"I have."

Silence.

"Can we talk later today?" he said. "I have a whole stack of data that needs attention."

She seemed disappointed but said it was okay.

*I've become quite adept at lying. A very useful skill, no doubt.*

For a successful career in finance you need three basic skills. Being able to bullshit and sound convincing, being able to lie without getting caught and stabbing innocent people in the back without feeling guilty. Anything else is secondary.

*Well, I got the first two down pretty good.*

He watched her walk away. Short skirt again. She wiggled her ass seductively when she walked. He wanted to fuck her now. He didn't care she was approaching fifty. She was so hot. The Paris trip had awakened something in him.

He didn't have time to pine over her any more. The reception called. The Indian guy had arrived and was waiting down in the main lobby. Hugo went down to the reception to fetch the temporary access card he had ordered for his guest. Then he went down to the lobby to get him.

"Call me Abi. My real name is Abhimanyu Hiranyagrbha, but seriously, no one can pronounce it. Not even me! Haha!" He had a thick Indian accent, the kind you hear when Indians appear as ethnic sidekick characters in Hollywood comedies. He was tall, much taller than most Indian people he had met, and he obviously paid anal attention to his appearance. Slick, combed hair, cleanly shaven except a very black and thick mustache and a suit and tie that looked very, very expensive.

190

He seemed intellectual, and on the way up he regaled Hugo about his university degrees from the US. Master in economics, Bachelor in economic history, even partial studies at the doctoral level. An overachiever. Hugo had heard that an Indian accent was a career stopper, but it sure as hell hadn't held Abi back.

They went up to the office and Hugo showed him the most basic of basics, the coffee machine and what buttons to push to get a decent cup. Then where the bathrooms were and then conference room three (the one which Hugo didn't use to write in, and the one Benzo didn't smash computers in) where he could hook up to the network and keep his stuff.

"What's the purpose of your visit?" Hugo asked.

"Oh, it's just a standard tour. I'm going to observe your business as part of a global streamlining effort to rationalize and realign the...." Blah, Blah, Blah. Hugo had become so allergic to financial gobbledygook that he sometimes automatically zoned out as soon as someone started talking. He was going to look at shit, that was enough for him.

He knew there was more to it, though. The gobbledygook was code. Bernie had laid it out for him many times. *Streamlining* and *rationalizing* was code for *cutbacks*, which in turn was code for *firing people*.

Bernie agreed when Hugo brought it up.

"US businesses have moved light clerical and customer services to India for quite some time now. We've also set up a call center in Portugal. I'd bet my house he has something to do with that. If I had a house, that is."

Hugo agreed.

During the first day he escorted Abi around the dif-

191

ferent departments and told him what they did. He introduced him to key people like managers and analysts who would be able to provide him with the data he needed. Abi was the most curious person he had ever met. The questions never stopped. FinCon, Risk, Customer Services, Marketing, IT, COB, everything. He asked about it all.

"What formula do you use to calculate your roll rates? How do you benchmark customer satisfaction? What's the current EBIT? How do you calculate ENR? How do you calculate ANR? How do you control that your quarterly RSA is delivered on time? Do you do quality reviews? What's your operational risk framework? Do you submit Basel II? What are your Collection Strategies? Do you use an external Collections Agency? How do your through-the-door numbers look? What are your write rates?"

*I can't believe I wasted so much of my valuable lifespan to learn all this shit.*

The questions continued during lunch, and when the guy finally quit Hugo felt faint. He had been ambitious in the days before the T-Rex and he had struggled to have at least basic knowledge about everything that went on in a bank. Good for Abi since he could then have all his questions answered, bad for Hugo because he had to answer them. His throat was all dried up. And it stole time away from the writing. Abi didn't seem affected at all. He was still full of annoying energy.

After a while the conversation shifted focus. No more bank technicalities.

"What's it like to work in London? Do you have a

family? What are your career goals?"

Hugo slid past most of the questions and lied about the rest. He didn't want to talk about such things and found himself wishing Abi would go back to the technical stuff.

At six p.m. Abi seemed to finally run out of steam. He asked how to get into town to the hotel. Hugo called a taxi at FastCredit's expense. They said goodbye and Hugo went home, all worn out. He wasn't used to having real stuff to do anymore.

The next day after lunch he lied and said he had something to do and that he'd be back in an hour. He just needed a break from all the questions. He went downstairs to get some air when he found Nella in the main lobby. She sat alone in the little sofa group where they sometimes had coffee together when they needed to get away. He joined her.

"You're happy today," she said.

He was in a good mood. He had been ever since Paris.

"Oh yeah, Nells. Hugo Melgren is back!"

"I can see that. What? Did the T-Rex get fired or something?"

"No. Alas."

In some strange way Hugo didn't want the T-Rex to get fired anymore. Why would he? Then he'd get a new boss and everything would go back to normal. Hugo didn't want his gray bank life back. He had started to enjoy the weird cat and mouse game he had with the T-Rex and the rest of the management team.

"In Paris," Nella said, "What happened with Katja?"

"What do you mean?"

"You know what I mean."

"Did I fuck her?"

"Yes."

"A gentleman never tells."

"So you did?"

He gestured that his lips were sealed. Nella turned away from him. She was angry for real. Another awkward silence. They didn't speak for a minute or so.

"Funny thing... the Indian guy seem to like me," he finally said just to break the silence. "He said that if I ever decided to keep wasting my life in a bank I should get in touch with him and he'd give me a reference. Well, he didn't use those exact words, of course. That's more my own interpretation." He smiled widely to make sure he communicated the sarcasm properly. Nella gave him a sour look. "Why do you always have to shit all over banking? There are people who actually find it worthwhile. Maybe you should look yourself in the mirror for once and see what it is you're doing?"

Hugo was taken aback, but when he thought about it maybe it wasn't such a bright idea taking a dump on that which a lot of people had made their life choice. He really didn't mean any disrespect for people who had made that choice. It was just wrong for him.

"I'm sorry, Nells. I didn't mean to hurt your feelings."

"No. You don't care about what others think."

"No, I don't care what *others* think. I care what *you* think."

"Then show it. Keep that shit to yourself."

She started walking for the stairs to the office.

"Come on...I'm sorry! Let's hug it out." He held out

his arms. "Come on now! Nells?"

"You know, this isn't some fucking book you're writing. This is real life. In real life people have feelings. They get hurt. This isn't a game." She started walking.

"Oh, come on Nells! Nellsy! Neeeellllsssyyyy!"

"I gotta go. I have to do those damn account transfers." She kept walking.

"Don't screw up!"

This time she didn't appreciate the teasing.

*Fuck. I'm an asshole.*

He let her go.

He sank down on the coach.

*What was that all about, anyway?*

Nella had always had objections to his rants about banking but she had never reacted this strongly. No, this was about Paris. Was she jealous? Why? They weren't together. They had agreed to be just friends.

Despite the attraction he felt for her, actually taking it any further was a thought he tried not to entertain.

*I'm probably reading too much into it anyway.*

He didn't have the energy to think about it anymore. He tried to focus on the novel. Some writing would keep his thoughts in line. He went back up and hoped he wouldn't run into Nella on the way. Things needed to cool down.

When he came back up Abi caught him again. He wanted to know more shit. This time about things Bernie did. He dumped Abi with him and went back to write. He had finished a whole chapter, covering his trip to Paris, when Bernie came up to him. He was bushed.

"Fuck, that guy has a lot of questions." He did an

195

impression of the Indian accent. "How do you do this? How do you do that? What controls? What data? What do you send? What do you report? What, what, what, WHAT!"

"Thank you and come again," Benzo said, also with an Indian accent. He had snuck up behind Bernie, the first time in a long while Hugo had seen him outside his IT workshop. He seemed happy.

"They decided to uninstall the encryption software," Benzo said. "The whole project was just a capital failure."

"Another one," Bernie added.

"So the Indian guy is killing you?"

"It's not so bad," Hugo said.

"Of course not," Bernie said. "He's bugging *me,* not you!"

"The question is, what the hell he is doing here?" Benzo said.

"Something is up," Bernie said. "I'm sure of it. He seems mostly interested in front office stuff. Sales, customer services. Something big is about to happen."

"You mean he's here to get acquainted with a business he's about to take over?"

"Exactly. That's why the chainsaw consultants were here. Outsourcing. They're moving the whole thing to India. Or maybe Portugal."

Neither Hugo nor Benzo disagreed.

Hugo went and got himself another cup of coffee. The fruit basket was a lot less luxurious now. Just a few half rotten apples (now without the little labels) and browning bananas. They were basically like that already when they came. He took a banana.

His head was empty again, but this time it was a good kind of empty. It felt like he had some control. He knew now what he was going to do. He was going to keep writing. FastCredit wouldn't be allowed to beat him. He wouldn't take Layla's offer. It would be like giving up.

After collecting his thoughts for a while longer he went to Layla's office to turn her down.

"Sure I can't persuade you?" she said, giving him a seductive look. She closed the blinds and locked the door.

"What'd you have in mind?" he said, against his better judgment.

She straddled him on the chair. Her miniskirt slid up over her hip, revealing her black thong.

*Oh crap! You had to provoke her, didn't you? Couldn't just have said no and left.*

She undid her blouse. Her belly was flat and he could see the distinct contours of her abs. She was fit like a young woman. No fat flaps, smooth skin. The only thing that revealed her age was some crow's feet and some deeper lines around the mouth. Maybe her slightly thinning lips. He noticed the barely visible vertical scar from her bellybutton down towards her crotch.

"That's right, dear. All C-sections. Everything is as it should down there. Nobody wants to fuck a glass of water, right?"

She undid his pants and grabbed his cock. With her other hand she pulled her panties aside. He was hard. She guided him towards her naughty bits and started rubbing the tip of his cock back and forth over her clit.

*AHHHH! What the fuck! This'll teach me to be careful*

*what I wish for, if nothing else.*

"You can come inside me," she said, while pressing the tip inside.

She put her hand back on his shoulder and really dug her nails in. It hurt like hell. The pain finally made him snap out of it. He pushed her back and put his cock back inside his pants.

"Very flattering," he said, fighting to gain his composure.

She climbed off him.

"Still no?" she said. She smiled.

"Yes. I'm afraid so."

She didn't seem angry. She just went to the door and unlocked it, showing him out.

When he came back to his cubicle he just sat down in his chair, exhausted, hoping that this wouldn't mean trouble down the road.

He took a sip of his now cold coffee and started writing. Almost fucking Layla would definitely go into the book.

"So what happened in there?" Benzo asked later during their coffee break. "The drapes were closed." He waggled his eyebrows suggestively, as if to say he knew something dirty went down in there. And of course it did.

"A gentleman never tells," Hugo said. Bernie said nothing. Nella was rolling her eyes.

"Oh come on!" she said. "Spill!" She seemed to have forgotten their fight from earlier. For that, Hugo was grateful. He didn't want to be on bad terms with Nella.

Hugo nodded no. "I won't tell. Although I do have

a question."

"What?"

"Okay. Hypothetically, let's say you dip the tip. You know what I'm saying? Does it count?"

Nella rolled her eyes again. "Come on, Hugo. You didn't?"

"No, no. No, no-oh-o! I'm not saying anything. Just a hypothetical."

"Hugs! You dawg!!" Benzo said. He raised his hand to high-five him. Hugo just stared at him.

"Don't leave a bro hangin', bro. That's not cool."

Hugo smiled. He looked around. Nella and Bernie weren't laughing. They were right. It wasn't cool. He slapped Benzo's hand.

"So? The tip?" he said again.

"You fucked her, dude," Nella said.

"No he didn't. It was just the tip. Tip doesn't *cunt*."

Hugo kept quiet while Nella and Benzo debated it.

"Tip counts!"

"It doesn't!"

"Hell yeah, it counts. *Cunt*. Ha! I just got that. But yeah, it counts. If it didn't you'd still be a virgin!"

That was a bit rough to say to Benzo. When Hugo thought about it, it wasn't too farfetched an idea that Benzo still was a virgin. But he didn't seem to take offense at that remark. Benzo had a good day today. Didn't seem so sensitive.

"Fuck you," he just said to her, smiling, with the middle finger raised. He was just full of confidence today. That was the first time Hugo had ever heard Benzo say something like that. Or made that gesture.

"Bernie, tell them. It counts," Benzo continued.

Bernie had said nothing up until this point. "I think Hugo exercised extreme self-control in this situation. No man I know, myself included, would've pulled away at that point in the process. Kudos to you, Hugo. Very strong."

"But what about the tip?" Benzo said. "Count or no count?"

Bernie sighed. "The benefit of the tip is that it counts if you want it to, and it doesn't if you don't. Those are the rules." He spat his gum and folded in a new one.

They all stared at each other for a moment.

"It counts," Nella said.

"It doesn't," Benzo said.

And so it went on.

That Friday it was time for yet another edition of *Couples Hell* in the shape of a dinner with Will and Sarah. They were child-free for the weekend, which apparently had made Will relapse into his former pain-in-the-ass pseudo-intellectualism. At least temporarily. He cited academic literature and threw about phrases in Latin all evening. The lame pedestrian ones everybody already knows, of course.

"*In vino veritas!*" he said while making a toast. The posh British accent only made it sound worse. "You have to seize moments like these. *Carpe diem!*"

He also seemed to have added another annoying trait. He had started correcting people whenever they said something. At least Hugo hadn't noticed it before. Maybe all the other annoying things had obscured it?

"Honey, can you get me a kleenex?"

"Sweetie, *Kleenex* is a brand name. These are generic. So it's technically a *tissue*."

Sarah was still in her IKEA mood and talked about kitchens and all the utensils they would be getting after their house was finally bought. Hugo found some solace in the fact that when they finally moved out to the burbs they would see a lot less of each other.

He spent the evening thinking about his novel. And the almost-sex with Layla. He managed to hide the marks on his back so far, although he had started questioning why he did so. So what if Jess found out? It's not as if Jess was putting out these days.

He added the occasional "mmh" and "I agree" at strategic places in the conversation to feign interest. Jess seemed happy here. She was back in her element where their problems didn't exist. Good for her. On the way home she talked happily about Will and Sarah's choice of brushed aluminum kitchen appliances and of all the pictures she had seen of the house they were bidding on. Hugo cringed when he thought of living like that but he wasn't in the mood for another boring future talk. He agreed instead. He still had no feelings of guilt. Not for Paris. Not for Layla.

**16**

After Hugo had said no to Layla he had a sudden back-
lash of guilty conscience. For a few days he felt com-
pelled to come in earlier in the morning. He did more
real work. He had no idea why. He didn't have to feel
guilty for discussing a new job. In fact it was least of
what he should fret about.

*Where's that flexible morality when you need it?*

He was still always almost an hour late so it wasn't
that bad when he thought about it. When he walked by
the T-Rex's office he didn't say hi. That would reveal
that he was just in. He just walked by with a fistful of
important papers, like he'd been here all along.

After tossing the important papers on his desk he
went to get a cup of coffee. It was unusually quiet today. He felt watched, as if everyone was onto his
scheme. He told himself that it was imagination.

He sat down to write but again he had a case of writer's block. His head was full of shit again. He gave up.

He needed a break. Something to purge all the fuck out. He needed to get away from FastCred.

He went to the kitchen to refill his coffee. He stopped by Nella's place on the way back.

"What's up, Nells?"

"Account transfers."

He noticed the infamous spreadsheet on her screen. It looked really convoluted. Numbers everywhere. Like a fly had been dipped in ink and then been allowed to run all over the screen. No colors or any other formatting to guide your eyes either.

"You sound hoarse," he said.

"I got some of the flu back. I have another week before it's gone again, I guess."

"You know what's good for the throat?"

She looked at him with that look. The one she always had when she was expecting something nasty. She was right, of course.

"Sperm," he said. "It will form a protective layer around your vocal chords. It's true. I read it in Scientific American. You can't argue with science."

She hit him in the side. She told him how work had bunched up after her illness and how she still hadn't caught up. "Miss a week in this place and you're fucked for six months." She had an impressive pile of papers and files on her desk. He got a glimpse of her inbox on her screen. It too was crammed full.

"I'm not particularly in the mood for wrestling with this," she said. Her breath smelled of mint from her lifesavers. She had been sucking on them since the first breakout way back. It wasn't annoying but a strikingly powerful scent this early in the morning. It was all

203

good, he guessed. It obscured the smell of diesel from the coffee.

"We could both use a break," Hugo said. "You know, we should just say we're sick and split."

"Yeah. That would be nice, Hugs. Really." She said it in such a way you could tell she wanted to but wasn't really prepared go through with it. But Hugo was.

"I mean it. We tell our bosses we don't feel well and then we get fuck out of here."

She stared at him as if she couldn't believe he was serious, like he had just told her he'd seen a UFO or something. Then she said: "You really use the f-word a lot these days."

He smiled. "That's what happens when you stop giving a...*fuck*!"

"I can't," she said and pointed to the pile of papers.

"What does it matter if you leave it another day? You'll never catch up anyway. This place is like fucking *Brazil*. Just endless bureaucracy and paperwork that doesn't really mean anything. We need a change of scenery, something colorful instead this gray shit. Let's take the tube to Hyde Park and slack off on the grass in front of Speakers' Corner."

It took a little persuading but she caved eventually. They decided to swing by her place to grab some blankets and a bottle of wine, maybe something to chew on. She lived only a few stops from Canary Wharf.

Well at her place he took the short tour of the apartment and then threw himself on the couch. He hadn't been here in at least a year and before then he couldn't remember. After he met Jess he couldn't hang out with Nells like this anymore. When you're in a committed

204

relationship you can't really have female friends any-more. At about that time Nells had also met... Matt, or whatever his name had been. It was over between them for some time now. Hugo had never asked any questions about it.

"I'm just going to change into something more park-appropriate," she said.

Hugo had a pair of dark jeans and a white standard model bank shirt. It would do.

Nella described her place as charming and cozy but admitted that the more appropriate terminology would be cramped and shitty. There was a distinct draft cutting through it. It was early October and still warm out, but her place was chilly for some reason. Every piece of furniture featured a blanket you could wrap around yourself to keep the cold out. Hugo tossed one over his feet. When it comes to living conditions, the United Kingdom is a third world country.

It was a one bedroom apartment with a kitchen so small it was probably in the Guinness Book of Records. It barely fitted the two-plated stove and a small shelf where she kept her laptop and a microwave. The bed-room sported a single bed, a closet and a really tiny IKEA chest of drawers. The closet door was open. It housed her overcoats and jackets and some cardboard boxes of unknown content.

*Not even spare room for a dildo.*

"I'll be right out," she said

"Take your time."

He turned on the TV.

Soccer. A highlight show where a panel of experts and viewers alike could call in and gripe about some player who had screwed up. Hugo didn't know who he was. It wasn't that Beckham guy.

*You're only as good as your last achievement.*

Nella was done. She had nice pair of tight, low cut jeans on. She even showed a little bit of whale tale. Hugo didn't mind. She tossed him an old sweater, probably one of Matt's old leftovers.

He managed to convince her to take the Tube this time. While Hugo did like the idea of sitting on the top floor of one of those funky London buses, it was so much slower. Besides, he liked the big city feel you got from taking a subway.

"A car would be nice," he said. "Even if you Brits drive on the wrong side of the road." He had never really felt he needed to adapt to that particular lunacy. Thankfully, you didn't have to with the 'look left, look right' painted on all the crosswalks.

"I've never had a car," Nella said. "Not even as a kid. My parents were Labour extreme. Socialists, really. They wanted me to use public transportation."

"They must have been so disappointed when you started working for a bank, capitalism's proudest institution."

"No. They were mostly proud."

"Hehe. It's easy to forget all about that socialist shit when you start making money. And now you're a middle-of-the-road liberal? A right-wing Labour sympathizer?

"Oh, sod off, will you! Not everyone can be a radical anarchist like you."

"I guess not."

They threw their blanket on the grass just opposite

Speakers' Corner. There was nobody at the mike right now but the massive lawn was reasonably crowded. That's what he liked about London—lots of people everywhere, all the time.

She cuddled up against him and rested her head on his chest. Her body lay at an angle out from his. Their sides didn't touch. It was innocent and intimate at the same time, exciting yet ordinary. He felt relaxed. At peace.

"This is nice," he said.

"Mmm."

"I think this is the part of the story where you fall in love with me."

She giggled. "We tried that, remember?"

"Yeah. But still."

She cuddled up closer.

"We could use a soundtrack. Too bad the real world doesn't work like the movies. Otherwise Nazareth's *Love Hurts* would be strumming along in the background by now."

Giggle. "Too cheesy. How about *Everything I do*. With Bryan Adams and those others?"

"Oh. Fuck no!"

More giggling.

"*Girl, You'll be a Woman Soon?*" he said. "Get a little *Pulp Fiction* groove going."

"Mmm. Yeah."

"Mmm, yeah. Diamond, though. Not Urge Overkill. I stick with the originals. Or Tommy James and Shondells. *Crimson and Clover*. Album version. The ultimate make-out song of the Sixties."

They sang. "Crimson and clover. Over and over.

Crimson and clover. Over and over."

"You have such old guy references, you know that?" Nella said.

"I know. I guess I was born out of sync with time."

She kissed his cheek. They fell silent for a while.

He thought about Paris again. Nella appeared to have put it behind her. If she ever was jealous, that is. He tried to clear his head and just enjoy the moment. They lay quiet for a long time while people came and went. Joggers were circling the huge lawn, others were having picnics and lunches, seated on the grass just like them. He didn't fall asleep. It was more like a meditative state. At least he thought so.

"You don't want kids, right?" Nella said all of a sudden. The question surprised him but didn't bother him.

"No."

"Why?"

"I don't know, exactly. I guess I've never really felt that... *calling*... everybody talks about. You know the one that drives you to procreate."

"And Jess?"

"She wants to, of course. Like everybody else."

He said that without feeling at all discomforted. Kids was a subject he and Jess avoided. They both knew they wanted different things and not talking about it was a way for them to plow through while hoping that other would have a change of heart. That would never happen. They both knew that too.

"I don't want kids either," she said. That surprised him. A woman past thirty not wanting kids. Biological clock a'tickin' and all. A lot of girls he had known had claimed they didn't want kids but they had all been in their early twenties. Few kept that view as the last of those precious eggs started dying.

"I'm so tired of having to defend myself," she said. "Lena, you know reception-Lena, asked me why I didn't have children during a break a few weeks ago and I told her the truth. That I didn't want any. The questions just started pouring out. Intimate questions. It's unbelievable that superficial acquaintances can get so nosy about stuff like that."

Hugo knew precisely what she meant. He had been subjected to it himself many times. Don't you love your girlfriend? Maybe you just haven't found the right one? Did you have a bad childhood? Were your parents unhappy? Who will keep you company when you're old? What if you change your mind?

Few people could understand why someone would choose not to do it, something that in their eyes is the very meaning of life itself. What if you regret *having* children? Nobody ever asks that question? You're not even *allowed* to ask that question.

"She said she felt sorry for me," Nella continued, "that I would never live to feel the joy of having a small child in my arms. How can I be sorry if I don't *want* that in the first place?"

"And then they lay the guilt trip on you," Hugo said. "You're not doing your duty towards society and the human race. Or to your parents who somehow acquired the *right* to a grandchild as compensation for giving birth to *you*. Or it's unfair to the unborn child itself who will never have the pleasure of being born. How can something be unfair to someone who doesn't even exist?"

"I have nothing against kids or people who have kids. Fuck as much you like, plop them out like ping pong balls, what do I care! I just don't see why they have to make me feel bad about my choice not to have any."

She nodded. "I think a lot of people wouldn't have children if they had the chance to think about it. The survival of the species depends on people conceiving before they have a chance to reflect too much over it. You hear all the time people saying that life doesn't have to change just because you have kids but then all you hear is how they suck the life out of them."

"Hehe! Well put! Maybe you should be the writer?"

She giggled. "Watch it. I might steal your readers."

"Yeah. What readers? But you're right. During the honeymoon phase they are all high on all those new parent emotions, brains flooded with oxytocin from the cuddle overload. Then you start to see that dead 'My GOD, what have I done?' look in their eyes. You know, when the kids are five, six years old and they can't find five minutes to themselves anymore between trips to the emergency room and soccer practice.

"They just realized they don't exist anymore except as child rearing drones. You're reduced to being the sidekick in your own life. Congratulations. Have fun with your stretched pussy and sagging tits. And the guys with their big blue ball sacks, swollen like a football because they haven't dunked it in the meat cave for two years straight."

"Now you're being mean. And disgusting."

"They started it."

She giggled again. Hugo laughed too.

The discussion faded away.  No more needed to be said.  After about an hour they started back, walking lazily along Oxford Street.  They had the rest of the day and there was no need to rush.

They eventually got hungry and stopped at a sandwich shop.  He had a BLT, she a spicy chicken.  They both had diet cokes.

Afterwards they went into Selfridges and shopped for clothes.  Nella found a blouse she liked.  A skimpy one, with a lot of cleavage and cut so that she would show her belly button.

"Get it," Hugo said.

"I don't know.  It's a bit too risqué for me, I think."

"Nonsense.  You'd look awesome in that.  Trust me."

"I know *you'd* like it.  You randy boy, you!  I guess it would be nice.  I need to dress more... you know... feminine, sometimes.  But I don't know, it's way too expensive."

It was a hundred and fifty.  Not prohibitively expensive for someone in their income bracket, but still nothing you'd joke about.

"Steal it!"

She giggled.

"I'm serious.  Do it."

"You *are* serious, aren't you?"

"Damn right!"

"Crazy idiot!"

She looked at the blouse, as if she was actually considering it.  Then she put it back on the shelf.

"Come on!  How often does something exciting happen in our boring office rat lives? Take the chance!"

He had to ask himself if he really was serious about it.

*I think I actually am!*

Ever since Paris he had felt a peculiar urge to stir things up. Not to be so nice and amicable all the time. Not to be such a pushover. He wanted to be *naughty*.

Nella gave him a confused look. Hugo took the blouse and stuffed it inside Matt's old sweater and started shoving Nella towards the exit. At the doors they waited until a large group of people crowded the entrance before deftly swooping outside the alarm pillar. The alarm went off anyway.

Nella flinched. He grabbed her before she could start running.

"Don't!" he said in her ear. "Just act perfectly normal. Follow the crowd and just start normally down the street."

Several of the other people started looking in their shopping bags, thinking it might have been them setting off the alarm. Security guards were slow but they came. By then Hugo and Nella were well down the street. Nobody followed them.

"You're out of your mind!" Nella half screamed when they were even further down and the tension had eased up a bit.

"Cool, huh?"

"Yes. It was, actually."

"Maybe we shouldn't do it again, though?"

She nodded.

They spent the rest of the day at Nella's place. They were mostly occupied with trying to pry the alarm off the blouse without damaging it. Those things are really tough but it caved eventually. He thought briefly, and involuntarily about making a move on her and from the look in her eyes, she seemed to want him to. Instead he exercised mind control and forced himself to think about other things. Fiddling with the alarm helped him concentrate.

When he stepped inside the door at home he was late. He expected to have to explain himself to Jess but she didn't ask any questions. He offered up a lie anyway—said he had been working late. Jessica just accepted it without demanding any details. They watched TV without talking much and went to sleep.

**17**

Today they had all been called to that nasty meeting they had been anticipating for a longtime. The cutback was here. The entire business was gathered in the big auditorium on the ground floor. Management had prepared a presentation. The first slide was already on display, featuring generic keywords floating around in little bubbles.

*Synergy, portfolio, optimization, road map, restructuring, reengineering, prioritization, up-selling, cross-selling, profitability, customer oriented, win-win, mindset, critical path, target audience, benchmarking, go-to-market, first-to-market, mark-to-market, process, e-business*

and of course *TEAM...*

Hugo stared at the screen. A virtual treasure trove of corporate Bullspeak.
　　*Team.*

It's always a *team* as long as you're useful. When you're not anymore, all of a sudden you're just an individual. Someone redundant. Someone you can throw away. Discard like yesterday's bread.

*Employers always demand loyalty of you but it never seem to work the other way around.*

The management team stood neatly in a row in front of the screen, in their navy blue suits. The rim of their jackets shone eerily in the light from the projector, like they were surrounded by an aura.

*Angels in navy blue.*

But they were not here to save anyone.

The T-Rex had been called in from Corporate, or wherever he spent his days. The entire business was gathered. Today it was game time.

"Too bad Bullshit Bingo is out," Nella said. "It was kind of fun, wasn't it?"

He and Nella sat in the back with Bernie in the row behind them. Bernie leaned forward.

"This is it, boys and girls. Behold, I saw a shiny navy blue suit. The man wearing it was Death. And hell followed with him."

On the stage Bryce went at it with a tsunami of generic team-building bullshit. He emphasized their collective responsibility. Everyone had to dig in and, Hugo supposed, he indirectly insinuated that everyone had part of the blame. If he was going down, he'd sure as hell take everyone else with him.

After blabbing on for a while about how the business was going turn everything around, as a *team*, he finally dropped the nuke. As an added insult he did it casually, sort of in passing, as if it wasn't a big deal. The entire

215

front office, everything directly related to customer contacts, was getting outsourced to Portugal. Hugo's new Indian friend Abi was going to head it.

"So I guess we know why he was here now," Hugo said. Nobody said anything. He turned to Bernie and they exchanged a *'told ya'* look. After the announcement it was dead quiet in the auditorium. Bryce ended it with wishing everyone good luck and then everyone returned to the office.

They all went to Bernie's place. It was decently private compared to most other cubicles, crammed away in a corner. As close to a corner office as you'll get without shoving your nose up the Big Man's stinkhole. Hugo was prepared for an onslaught of shit thrown at management. From the looks of it so were Nella and Benzo. They looked utterly surprised when he just sank heavily down into his chair and exhaled. No barking, no clever words of wisdom. They were all just silent.

"For moments like these," Bernie finally said, while he started digging in his bottom desk drawer, "you need something strengthening."

He dug out a flask, not the old steel one he normally used, but a nicer one. Silver, with gold carvings. "I got it from some former colleagues." He held it up. "Lagavulin, for special occasions."

The cap wasn't attached to the flask as with many other models. He screwed it off and used it as a glass. He held up a quiet toast and knocked it back. He poured another one and passed it to Hugo.

"Don't mind if I do," Hugo said.

"*Noch ein koch, bitte!*" Bernie said.

"What?"

"It's fake German for 'another cap', please. We used to toast that way on our binge drinking trips to Germany back in the early Nineties."

"You know that if the bosses see you they'll have your arses," Nella said.

"I don't think there will be much barking today," Bernie said.

"And what difference does it make?" Benzo said.

"I'm going back to my desk," Nella said. She left with a brisk walk.

"What's up her bum?" Benzo said. "We haven't done anything. Have we?"

"She's angry," Bernie said. "It's perfectly understandable. We all react differently to news like this."

"She's not angry with us," Hugo said. "I'd better go talk with her."

He left after her without noticing he still had the flask in his hand.

"You okay?" he said when he caught up.

"No. I'm not. Who is on a day like this?"

It was a stupid question. It's just something you say.

"Don't worry about me," she said. "I just need some alone time. Digest it. We'll talk later. Okay?"

"Sure?"

"Yes. Go back to Bernie. You still have the flask in your hand. If the bosses see you..."

"I don't give a crap."

The cap was still at Bernie's. He took a sip directly from the flask. He coughed. Lagavulin really is powerful smoky.

"Okay," he said. "I'll go. But if you need to talk let me know."

"Same to you."

Hugo handed Benzo the flask when he came back. He poured himself a cap and drank it.

"We made it this time," he said. "But this isn't the end of it, is it?"

They both looked at Bernie. He seemed bothered for once, to be everybody's mentor.

"No. It isn't."

Hugo went back to his desk. A thick fog of despair had crept in over the entire office. It was like at a funeral. Nobody was working. Some were sitting by themselves, some in groups. Some were even crying.

In the front a young guy exploded and shoved all the things on his desk down on the floor.

*Toby? Is that his name?*

He was one of the cool Generation X types who wore discreet make-up and had gross amounts of product in his hair. Then the guy walked confidently towards the management team's hallway. Maybe to ream them out, tell them to go fuck themselves. One could always hope.

Some of the girls were hugging and crying. These were all people Hugo knew, even if he didn't have a close relationship with them. In a short while none of them would be here anymore.

In the back office everyone was silent, as if honoring their fallen comrades with a genuine minute's silence. Hugo sank down into his chair.

Even if he wasn't affected directly he felt for all of his co-workers. And in advance for everyone who was going to be next. For a moment he slipped back into his former self, the placid office guy who did everything asked of him. The one who wanted security and a respectable career. The guy he was trying to kill. Some moments had been good here. Even if it was a long time ago. He snapped out of it and when he did, he felt more determined than ever to write the book. Besides, he had just acquired new material.

## 18

It didn't take long before the entire front office was deserted. The desks and computers were still there. It was an office cemetery where the desks were graves and the black computer screens the headstones. It was dead silent. No voices, no buzzing printers, no tapping from keyboard keys. A monument to what once was.

Back office wasn't as quiet, not as dead, but the pace had dropped considerably. All reporting linked to front office activities had ceased and moved to Portugal. Everything was just gone. Only Finance, Marketing and Legal still had same workload. There simply wasn't anything left to do at FastCredit and many of Hugo's co-workers had started looking for other jobs. The crisis made sure they weren't going to find any.

Hugo's own routine hadn't changed. He came around ten, ten-thirty. Left his coat in the basement, grabbed a bunch of important papers and went up to the office. There the music from his internet radio already played, his screen showed slides of his work-related software, his jacket hung over the back of his chair.

He was heading for the printer room when he saw the Rex thundering towards him. Hugo froze for a second. He didn't know what to do. The Rex hadn't seen him yet but if he did he'd know Hugo came in late. Again. There was no way he was going to talk to that fucktard now. He was on a roll from this morning. His fingers bled inspiration. Creativity dies a violent death when it comes into contact with the likes of banking dinosaurs.

The T-Rex stopped and looked around, scanning over the walls of the cubicle landscape, his nose in the air as if he was trying to *sniff* Hugo out. Even from this distance Hugo could see the nostrils flaring. Then the T-Rex continued towards the printer room. Hugo ducked and threw himself in behind a cubicle wall.

*Why the fuck did I do that for?*

It was a reflex. A damned stupid one.

*I could've just backed up into the printer room and waited, sneak out when he left.*

The printer room had two exits. There was no way he would've been caught if the T-Rex decided to take a look in there. Now he was on the floor. On all fours, with some pages from the novel locked in his jaws. It would look pretty silly if the T-Rex came around the corner now, finding him here like this. Luckily the office was decently empty. No one else had seen him. Yet.

Hugo peeked carefully around the corner of the cubicle wall. Rexie was on the move. He sort of half *skulked* around, slightly hunched over, almost tip-toeing. Like Batman shadowing a crook. Not the cool Batman. The fat one from the goofy sixties TV series.

*Na-na, na-na, na-na na-na...*

He caught a break. Rexie went the other way. That meant he had a chance. Escape somewhere, dump the pages and come back in like nothing had happened. He quickly crept past an opening to the next section.

Bernie's cubicle was close by. A stopover at Bernie's would provide him with a legitimate reason for being away from his desk. He crept along to where the wall split into another hallway, looked to his right towards the front office section. Clear. Then to the left towards the conference rooms in the back.

And there he was. Rexie had somehow worked his way around him. At the moment his back was towards Hugo, temporarily distracted by a colleague who had engaged him in what seemed to be idle office conversation. The fake laughs gave it away. Hugo backed up behind the wall again.

The hallway he was about to cross led to Benzo's cubicle. He couldn't stay there, though. It would look strange to be there with nobody else around. Benzo was still occupied in his conference room-slash-IT-chop-shop, cleaning up the aftermath of the failed encryption software installation. And the rage therapy he had applied to the machines with the hammer. But it could serve as a temporary hideout until the T-Rex got tired of this and returned to his office.

The conversation with the colleague droned on and on. Hugo was stuck where he was. His palms and knees had started to burn intensely against the poop-colored carpet. He had started to drool a bit as well since he couldn't swallow properly with all that paper in his mouth. He wouldn't be able to hold out much longer.

*I could make a run for it?*

If he ran quickly, and stealthily he could make it across to Benzo's cubicle unnoticed. The T-Rex still had his back turned against him.

*Come on! Three quick steps. And maybe a dive. That's all it takes.*

He backed up a few feet to get a running start and ran crouched along the cubicle wall. When he passed the corner and out into the hallway he could see in the corner of his eye that the colleague had left and that the T-Rex was turning around towards him. In just a tenth of second he would see him. Instinctively he dove into Benzo's cubicle, like a soldier throwing himself out of the way of an exploding grenade. He bit down hard around the papers to keep them from flying about. When he landed he rolled to break the fall, hitting his knee hard against the metal leg of Benzo's desk. He must have hit a nerve—the pain was so intense he almost fainted. He backed up under the table and hoped he hadn't caused too much of a ruckus.

He waited.

Waited.

Waited.

No T-Rex.

He crawled out from under the table, stood up slowly and peeked over the cubicle wall. No one. Luckily, it was a quiet day with a lot of people were out of the office. If anyone had seen him crawl around like that questions would have had to be asked. Nobody does weird stuff like that in an office, except in movies of course.

He got up, straightened out his shirt, took the papers out of his mouth (and wiped off the drool casually against his leg) and then proceeded as normally as he possibly could towards Bernie's. His knee pulsated with pain but it was only a few more feet. He sank down in Bernie's extra chair and exhaled.

"What's going on, kid?" Bernie was chewing his gum. He didn't look up from the screen, which probably meant he wasn't working. He was looking at something funny and laughing on the inside.

"You survived by a cunt hair," Bernie said, still not looking up.

"What do you mean?"

Now he looked up. "The T-Rex and Bryce tried to get you fired. Some even-higher-ups stopped them."

"Remind me to send them a fruit basket."

Bernie nodded and smiled. "It's against policy to fire people without due process."

"Saved by bureaucracy. Irony can be pretty ironic sometimes." He got up to go back to his cubicle. It was probably safe now.

"Be on your toes," Bernie said as he stepped outside the cubicle. "Frank really seems on fire. What's with the leg, by the way? And why are you out of breath?"

He told him.

"Okay," Bernie shrugged. "See you."

He made it all the way to his cubicle without any trouble. The T-Rex was nowhere to be seen at the moment. He sank down in his chair and closed his eyes.

*Okay, see you? That's it, after a story like that?*

Crazy stuff was becoming so commonplace that nobody even reacted anymore. It was like nothing had happened.

Maybe Nella was right. It didn't happen. It was just part of the book and he couldn't tell the difference between what was real and what was fiction anymore. He thought about Layla and the dip of the tip. How crazy was that?

*Maybe it didn't happen? I mean, how often do things like that really happen? Real life is boring. Uneventful. You know, with the cornflakes every morning, the Tube, the paper shuffling, the moving of decimals, the Tube again, day in and day out. Office work. Dinners in couples hell, IKEA, brushed aluminum kitchen appliances. There is no magic. No miracles. No God. No time travel. No Narnia. No Kingdom of Oz. Just plain ol' fucking Kansas where nothing ever happens.*

At this very moment he was genuinely not sure if the incident with Layla actually happened or if it was some fantasy he thought up for the book. It scared him.

*Nawh! Of course it happened! Didn't it? Mommy....I'm scared.*

He dropped it. He had no time for crap like that. He had a problem. The T-Rex was on his ass. Bernie was right. Hugo had noticed that the T-Rex had started showing up at his cubicle at odd times, probably to see if he was there or not. He had started to request details about what Hugo did, or what he thought he did. Hugo's only real assignment was that damn audit which had been postponed several times now due to the layoffs and the crisis, twice on his own initiative.

There was a new world order in FastCredit now and nobody could get a grip on it. It was an excellent time for bullshitters like Hugo to make it seem like he had tons of work. If only the T-Rex could stay away it would all be gold.

Hugo and Nella spent more time together down by the sofa group in the main lobby. They talked about the good ol' days, their college years and the first years at FastCredit. Nostalgia is a comfortable sanctuary.

"You were right," Nella said.

"About what?"

"Everything. Management. They really screwed up."

"They're idiots."

She looked tired. She never said anything but Hugo guessed she'd started hating working in the bank as much as he did.

"Time to go back up?" she said.

"Pretend to work a little bit more and then head on home."

"I can't. I actually still have tons of work."

He felt for her. Spending energy working for a business that probably wouldn't even be here in a few months' time seemed like an utter waste.

"How's the book coming?"

"Fine."

She looked at him intensely and then gave him a kiss on the cheek. "You know, Hugs, with you and me? It'll never be off the table. You know that, don't you?"

"I know."

She gave him another kiss, on the lips. No tongue. They held it for a while. It was sweet and very sensual. Then she got up and went back to the office.

Later that afternoon the T-Rex wanted to see him for an update. Hugo prepared himself for a burst of creative lying about the streamlining project and the audit, and hoped he wouldn't get anything new on his agenda.

The T-Rex sat a long time without saying anything, as he always did. He did his Mr. Burns thing. Hugo lost his patience and started spewing the lies.

"I'm still collating materials for the audit. And I'm making some headway with the streamlining of the reports. It's harder now with the front moved to Portugal, but even more necessary now when the channels have changed again."

The T-Rex said nothing.

*What the fuck is wrong with him? He's trying to psych me out.*

He kept up the bullshit for a while longer. The T-Rex appeared to be listening but still didn't say anything. Now it was getting truly uncomfortable. Many minutes passed before the T-Rex finally leaned forward in his chair and started talking.

"I can't get a grip on you," he said.

Hugo hesitated.

*What the fuck does that mean?*

"What is it that you do here?" he said.

"Well," Hugo said. "I just told you, didn't I?"

"Don't be coy. Do you really think you can pull a fast one on me? I don't know what exactly it is that you do here these days but I intend to find out. You're never at your desk. Never. I've looked around the other departments and you're not there either."

Hugo's heart was pumping now. He told himself it didn't matter if he got caught. It was just part of the game. He reminded himself that he was a new person now. Someone who doesn't give a fuck. It helped a little, but it's hard to change your personality overnight. His body still reacted as the scared little security-jonesing office clerk he tried to kill. Flight mode. Adrenaline. Raised pulse. It doesn't matter what the rational part of your brain is trying tell you.

"I...don't know what you mean," he said, trying to sound unaffected. "Sometimes I need to get away from the buzz and I go to one of the conference rooms."

"No. There's something off with you. You're not producing any results on what you say you do. I haven't seen anything."

"That's quite a serious accusation there. I don't know what you're talking about."

"You told Bryce you started a project during my absence. Do you have anything to show for it?"

"Of course."

"Then do it."

*Fuck.*

There was nothing, of course. At least he didn't seem to know about the writing.

"I'm keeping my eyes on you from now on. I want to see everything you've done. And the audit too. You have until Thursday. Then I want it on my desk."

Their cold war had turned hot. The equilibrium had shattered. Now he had to do something. Take *action*.

He of course started by consulting the old-timer. Bernie would know what to do.

"Okay," Bernie said. "Let's just keep cool here."

"I am cool."

"Oh. Okay. How much have you done with audit?"

Hugo told him he had marked a couple of binders with last year's audit materials that he had re-dated.

"Good. Keep doing that. It won't take long for you to do the rest. Old Rexie won't notice. It's not in his job description to review the stuff, just collect it. He'll flip through it, but won't go deep enough to expose you."

"Yeah. Most of it is outside his area of expertise anyway. He won't look at that."

"And the audit itself won't happen for a while yet so you'll have lots of time get the real stuff together if that should ever be needed. With a little luck it will be permanently canceled due to all the shit that's been going on here."

"The...hmm...*initiative*?"

"Yes. It was about streamlining the reporting chain, was it not?"

"Yes."

"Okay. So flowcharts would be something that could interest him, right? They look complicated and it always seems like there's a lot of hard work behind them."

Hugo agreed. A full set of nice looking flowcharts would probably placate the Rex. The problem was that he didn't have any. Of course he hadn't counted on actually having to make some.

"No problem. We'll simply produce some."

Bernie smiled enthusiastically. Hugo suspected he was secretly envious of his scheming. Bernie too had cheated himself through a whole career but never in such an organized and premeditated fashion.

"It takes time to make all of those charts," Hugo said. "Maybe I could throw some bullshit together and show him. Hope he buys it. But that would defeat the purpose of the entire scam. There's a principle involved here!"

"Agreed. But you don't have to make them. I have a bunch of flows from my old job. I got them from a friend who still works there. Change the logo to Fast-Credit's and some other strategic information and the T-Rex will never know the difference. They all look the same no matter where they come from. Banks are very much alike."

Bernie brought the flowcharts up on the screen. They were different but surprising little so. It would work like a charm.

*Some changes here. Some there. BANG! Done and DONE!*

It was perfect and wouldn't take more than an hour or so.

"He won't call your bluff even if he should suspect something," Bernie said. "He's too scared to look like a jackass. Besides, this is basically what it actually looks like."

Hugo nodded.

"If he finds something that doesn't add up I'll just say that it's one of those things that I was hoping to improve. It's airtight."

"He wanted a war...," Bernie said with a big smile.
"... so he'll get one!"

The T-Rex dropped in a little later that afternoon.

"I'm leaving now," he said, calmly as if the morning's declaration of war had never taken place. "I have a meeting with my insurance company about my vacation home. It burned down, remember?"

Hugo nodded.

"See you tomorrow," the T-Rex said and left.

Around three Hugo took a break in the lobby with Bernie and Nella.

"I can't get a grip on the old bastard," Hugo said. "One moment he is virtually psychotic and the next he is almost *nice*. He's like an idiot-savant, but without the savant part."

"But he *is* right to suspect something, isn't he?" Nella said with a smirk.

"Yes. But he's acting like he already knows. Which he doesn't."

"How could a guy like him go so far as to become a manager?" Nella said. "I mean, he's obviously some kind of mild sociopath."

"*The Jacket Trick*," Bernie said. "Everyone who gets somewhere in this business does it. You bullshit, you lie, you learn to talk the talk, you make sure you say all the right buzzwords to convey the image that you are someone who knows something. You dress up in fancy suits and then you kiss the right ass and kablammo! You're the boss somewhere. The perverse beauty of it all is that nobody will ever call your bluff because they're all pulling the same stunt! It's sort of a Nash equilibrium for cheaters."

"An equilibrium of bullshit," Hugo said. "That's beautiful! And a *Nash* equilibrium, no less. Not just a regular one. Wu-huuu! Fancy Schmancy."

"I have my moments."

"Admit it, you just heard it from *A Beautiful Mind*, didn't you."

"Yeah."

"So all managers are assholes?" Nella said.

"I suppose there are exceptions that prove the rule. But in this business people are attracted to power and money. Incorruptible people are attracted to other things in life. If you've never encountered a Frank T. Rex, you probably *are* a Frank T. Rex."

Hugo laughed.

"What exactly are these non-bullshitters attracted to?" Nella asked.

"Fucked if I know. I'm not one of them. I cheat. But not for power and money but to get out of having to work so I can focus on my drinking and womanizing."

Nella stared at him.

"What? I didn't make the world the way it is. I'm just trying to get through it as cleanly as possible."

Bernie took a sip from his coffee, which was enhanced by a little vodka from his flask (not the good one). "Hugs, here," he said. "He's not like me. He has ambitions. I would've never tried writing a book in his situation. I'd just slack off and go home early."

Hugo laughed. "But I cheat."

"Yeah, but for a good reason."

"Maybe I should use my time to work on my drinking too?"

"I have all the good stuff up in my drawer. The key is under the keyboard."

"Thanks. I'll remember."

Bernie gave him a friendly pat on the shoulder and they went up again.

## 19

The T-Rex was serious when he said he'd keep an on eye on Hugo. Never before had he taken that many strolls through the office, passing by Hugo's cubicle. It felt like the T-Rex's eyes were on him wherever he hid.

That Thursday when the T-Rex wanted all the stuff delivered didn't begin well when Hugo was caught trying to sneak in undetected at eleven. The T-Rex played twenty questions.

"Where have you been?"

"I was in Finance helping out with their Basel II reporting."

"I didn't see you there."

"We were in a conference room."

"I checked them. You weren't there."

"When were you there? We went downstairs to get some coffee after a while."

The T-Rex eyed him. Up and down. It was really weird, as if he was trying to find some physical evidence that Hugo had been up to no good. Like what? Grass stains from slacking off on a lawn somewhere? Bedhead? The T-Rex sighed heavily when he couldn't find anything.

"Four hours," the T-Rex said and pointed to his watch. "Then I want to see everything on my desk."

Hugo was working on modifying the flowcharts Bernie had given him. He was already done with the audit files. The flowcharts presented more work than he had, though. He had planned to write in the morning before coming in but realized that there simply wasn't enough time. The writing had to wait. It wasn't just about writing a book anymore. It was personal. He *wanted* to beat the T-Rex now, win the game. And the game had to take precedence for now. No fucking dinosaur was going to eat Hugs Melgren.

The charts had to be perfect. A single slip-up, one little box referring to the wrong thing and the illusion would be shot. It would've almost been more efficient to do the charts from scratch, but of course there was a principle involved. No real work.

After working for three hours he was finally approaching the finish line. He decided to go through them again just to be sure but first he needed a break.

He thought about trying to squeeze in a few paragraphs on the novel but he was all out of juice. Fiction writing wasn't as taxing as doing corporate bullshit work but it was still too much right now. Besides, with the T-Rex on the prowl he faced an increased risk of getting caught.

He decided to take a stroll. He went to Nella's desk first but she was in a meeting. Her workload was still extremely high since the outsourcing. Moving a few departments is more work than it sounds. And it sounds like quite a lot. Hugo was more grateful than

T-Rex had cut him off from most of the real
The man's paranoia was working to his ad-
.age every once in a while.

Benzo was out sick again so there would be no idle
chit-chat with him. Flu, again, although Hugo knew
what the real problem was. He ended up with Bernie as
usual.

"I don't have anything to do anymore either," Bernie
said. "They're not telling me anything. I'm simply playing dead to see if anything happens. So far nothing."

Bernie drank the last of his coffee from the disgusting cup that he never cleaned. He folded in a new Juicy
Fruit. "Did you notice?"

"What?"

"I think the staff is splitting into two groups. Two informal groups, that is. Have you noticed how some
have a lot of work on their desks while others don't?
How some people are walking around with an odd confidence while others seem depressed?"

He had noticed, now that he thought of it.

Bernie went on. "I think we're looking at another run
of the chainsaw. Some back office positions have become redundant after the outsourcing and I'll bet the
house I'll never own it's already decided which ones.
Not officially, of course, but it's been settled already."

"You mean the ones who will get to stay already
know?"

"Exactly. That's where the confidence comes from."

"Then we're out, I guess."

"Yes. I guess we are."

Bernie got up. "Speaking of which, I have something
to tell you."

"What?"

"Not here. Let's go down to the lobby."

They took a detour past the kitchen to see if there was something to chew on. Fruit baskets and afternoon snacks had become a rarity lately. It was empty this time as well.

They made their way downstairs. Hugo anticipated some more juicy stuff about management or some other gossip. Maybe Bryce was finally getting axed?

They sat down in the couch, which was empty as always. Bernie paused a little too long before speaking. The kind of pause you take when you're about to say something uncomfortable.

"I'm leaving," Bernie finally said. "My last day is this Friday."

Hugo was stumped. Of all the things he had expected Bernie to say that was the last thing on his mind. He had viewed Bernie more like a fixture, as part of the building, not like an employee. He had been with Fast-Credit since the beginning of time as far as Hugo was concerned. But now that it was said it was just all too obvious. Bernie's career here was, just as Hugo's, soon over under any circumstances. It was really just self-evident that he would move on.

"Okay," Hugo said. "New job?"

"Same job, different bank. Loan Depot. One of my buddies knows the CEO there and he got me in. Same guy who gave me the flowcharts."

"Why are you leaving so soon? What about your notice period?"

"I'll be placed in quarantine. Apparently they fear I might sneak away with some vital business secrets.

Why anyone would want to steal something away from this fucked up place is beyond me."

"Yeah. Worst bank ever. And when I say ever, I mean eeeeeh-ever."

"So a little bit of down time for you?"

"Yes. Haven't I earned it?"

"Not really."

They both laughed.

"I'm sorry to lose you," Hugo said.

"We'll stay in touch."

Hugo nodded. You always say that when someone leaves but you never really do.

"Who will teach me tricks now?"

"I have nothing more to teach you. You're the master now. You've even surpassed me. I've never done anything like you have. So thought out. So organized. "

"When I met you I was but the learner…"

They smiled, but didn't laugh. They went back up. It was time to meet the T-Rex. Hugo was tired and still unsure about the accuracy in the charts. He would have to chance it.

The T-Rex sat and stared at the fifty-something flowcharts Hugo had prepared. He was looking very thoroughly.

When Hugo first put them on the desk the T-Rex had seemed surprised, as if he had expected that nothing would be delivered. Maybe he had even expected Hugo to confess what he'd been up to. When Hugo didn't he was clearly disappointed.

After a few very long minutes he finally looked up from the papers. He was clearly frustrated, hopefully because he couldn't find any errors.

"What about the audit?" he said.

"They're done. All the binders are in conference room one. You can inspect them at any time."

The T-Rex grunted under his breath, barely audible.

"And this?" He pointed to the flowcharts. "What's this going to result in?"

"It's an overview of the reporting chain all the way up to global level."

The T-Rex flipped through some of them again.

"Okay," he said. "They look good. I'll look at them more closely later."

It looked like the T-Rex didn't have anything else to say. Hugo got up to leave.

"Remember," the T-Rex said as Hugo reached the door, "I'm still keeping my eye on you."

Hugo smiled, a smile with just a hint of defiance, and then went back to his cubicle. He felt satisfied. Great, even, but he reminded himself that this was just a temporary victory at best. The T-Rex would be on his ass until he found something. The game was still on.

He wrote the rest of the day, full of energy inspired by all the new events. The T-Rex kept away, hopefully sulking in his office like a little kid who's been denied candy from mommy and daddy. But more likely, he was fine-combing the flowcharts, eager to pounce on any discrepancy.


Later that afternoon Nicolas called and wondered if he was up for a beer at *The Tick*. It wasn't time for their regular intake yet but it was fine. Hugo could use a bit of alcohol to expunge the crap clogging his mind. He asked Nella but she didn't have time to spare. She was pulling overtime with the dangerous money transfers. Apparently things weren't adding up.

"It's something with the write offs that's not right," she said. "New York wants the results submitted by Friday so I have to get it done by then."

"Let me know if I can do something," he offered.

"Sure. Thanks."

Nick was already at the bar. Their usual table was taken. Lardy only reserved on their regular Wednesdays. It was a couple, a kind of cute chick and a balding fat guy, not totally unlike George Costanza. Hugo went over to them. He pulled Nicolas along with him for support. He banged his palms against the table.

"Get the fuck away from our table." He gave the guy the crazy eyes and pointed to the reservation sign Lardy always put there.

"What...?"

He growled. "Doode, don't make me ask twice."

"Okay, okay..."

They got up and left. The chick looked terrified, the guy had a mix of fear and defiance in his eyes but he never challenged them.

"Fuck, Hugs! What's going on with you?"

"I don't know."

"Guess I'm buying today, huh?"

"Sure."

Nicolas laughed. "You need to chill." He changed the subject. "I could leave early for once. It's starting to look like crap for us now too. It's all falling apart."

"I know. I experienced the same thing a few months ago, remember?"

The both sighed and took a sip, almost in perfect tandem.

"So what's going on with you?" Nick asked.

Hugo told him about the T-Rex's overt declaration of war.

"You should kick his ass."

"Say what?"

"Just what I said."

Hugo nodded, a little surprised. Nick hadn't exactly been on his side the last few months. But he guessed the events of late could break even the most hardened skeptic.

"I hate banks," Nicolas said.

"Amen."

They drank.

When he got home that night Jess was in the kitchen waiting for him. She had packed a bag.

"I'm staying with my parents for a few days," she said.

Hugo nodded.

"I think you need some time to think," she continued. "Get your act straight."

"So you're going away to remind me that if I continue along this road it will have consequences? For us?"

She looked down. "If you want to put that way, then...sure. I'm not seeing a particularly bright future the way we're going."

He sighed. He had been putting it off for way too long. It was time for the talk.

"Look, Jess, why don't we just cut the crap? We both know this isn't working anymore."

Her eyes saddened.

"I'm sorry...," he started.

"Fuck you! We're not breaking up. We're not ending this because you have some childish idea about being a writer."

"Childish?"

"Yes! You're a big baby. Grow up!"

"Okay! So fine. It's childish. I am a child. Trapped in a man's body. I admit it. But I am who I am. I'm not going to change. I tried for years to be just another office rat but I can't do it. I just can't."

She grabbed a plate from the sink and threw it at him. He ducked and it slammed against the wall and broke.

"Fuck you! This wasn't supposed to happen. We were going to have a family together. We were happy!"

She was crying now but it was at least partly tears of rage. He walked up to her and held her. She didn't resist.

"That's the thing," Hugo said. "I never was happy. I was being forced into this mold of someone I don't want to be. Someone I *can't* be."

"It'll be different when you get a new job. You'll change your mind."

"No, Jess. This is real life. It's not some Hollywood rom-com where the slacker pulls his act together in the third act and realizes he's really all about family values and shit. I am what I am. I won't change."

She looked down on her feet. "So many years wasted."

She didn't say anything else. There was really nothing more to talk about. This was a long time coming. They both knew it.

"It wasn't a waste, Jess. We had some very good times. A relationship is not necessarily a failure just because it doesn't last for an entire lifetime."

They spent most of the night talking, crying, holding each other, remembering, reasoning, rationalizing. When daylight broke through the windows they both decided it was time. Jess got up, put her coat on and grabbed her bags.

"I'll be back for my stuff later," she said.

"Take whatever time you need."

They hugged one last time and she was gone. Hugo went to the liquor cabinet and poured himself a whiskey. It was done. Now he finally felt guilty.

**20**

He called in sick and slept the entire next day but the day after that he felt better. Great, even. Like another ton of bricks had been lifted off his shoulders. He knew the prudent thing would be to feel bad about breaking up with Jess for at least a while longer but he just didn't. He still loved her in a way, or at least he *cared*, but it was a different kind of emotion from what it once had been. She would be happier without him. His inner manchild just held her back. It was never fair to her.

Or to him. He had been doing a version of the jacket trick long before Bernie told him about it. He had pretended to be someone he wasn't. He would never feel at home in the world of high finance or suburban family life. He would never be that guy. He was a writer. A fucked up tale spinner. A systematic and obsessive liar. One that wrote those lies down and hammered them into stories.

Jess would be all right. In real life broken hearts always mend with time. There's no such thing as soul mates or lifelong love. No Harrys and Sallys. No Romeos and Juliets. No Meg Ryans and Tom Hanks.

There are no happy endings that last. There's only the passage of time and the withering of emotions, no matter how overwhelming they had once been. Cynical, maybe, but in his experience, real life was always gray scale. That's why he escaped into fiction.

He met Nella in the lobby.

"You okay?"

"Why wouldn't I be?"

"You don't look okay."

Really? She had probably confused his thinking face with his sad face.

"I left Jess. But I'm okay."

"What? You poor thing."

She hugged him. "Let's talk."

"I'm okay," he reassured her.

"Of course you're not okay! You just broke up. You must be devastated."

"I'm not. It was for the best."

She kept hugging him and insisting that he wasn't okay for quite a while longer, as if it was an impossibility that he actually was. It would've been for most people, he guessed, but he wasn't most people. He was Hugo fuckin' Melgren. Or maybe he wasn't okay? Maybe he was just in shock. Maybe he'd come crashing down later when the dust settled.

They still spent an hour talking. About Jess, about FastCredit, the crisis. When he got up to his desk he made an extra effort to push all that aside and reminded himself of what was important.

*Just keep writing the book. Screw FastCred out of as many salaries as possible and take down the T-Rex.*

He had to stay alive until he was included in the next

mass sacking. That way he would get a nice severance package to kick off his new slacker-slash-writer lifestyle. If he was caught before then, he would get fired for negligence. That meant no money.

There was goodbye cake in kitchen two for Bernie. Management had bought a huge ice-cream/chocolate cake. Bernie had, just like Hugo and Natalie before, never been part of that little group of favored protégés surrounding Bryce. But on a personal level he was loved by everyone, including the rest of management.

"Screw it all," Bernie whispered and scooped in a big chunk of cake. "In two hours I'll have completed my hand-overs and then I'm out. Never to set my foot in this sorry excuse for a bank ever again."

"Well, good luck," Nella said.

People flowed through, taking a piece while it lasted, said bye to Bernie and then disappeared gain. It took an hour or so for the whole business to go through the procedure.

Bryce was there. He was talking to Fredrick, the customer services head. That very customer services that was now in charge of these days.

"Nothing," Bernie said. "He's just here to make sure everything is handed over okay. A task that's probably done by now. He'll leave soon enough."

"Or get fired," Nella said.

"No," Bernie said. He spoke quietly so that nobody would over hear. "People at that level never get fired. They simply *leave*. Worst case scenario they are asked to step down of their own accord. Either way they're always safe from the negative consequences a sacking might have. They can move on in their careers as if nothing ever happened, even if they were the ones who screwed up."

When Bryce was finished with Fred he came up to them.

"So you're leaving?" he said, with slightly, but still clearly noticeable, cynical tone. "I guess good luck is in order."

The two shook hands. They exchanged an intense look.

"What was his problem?" Nella said when Bryce left.

"He sees Bernie as a traitor," Hugo said.

"Yes," Bernie said, "if you leave of your own accord that's exactly what you are. Funny, but the same logic doesn't seem to apply in reverse when companies fire you."

"You're not a team player if you leave," Hugo said.

Bernie chuckled. "In the world of banking, being a team player means that you do what the hell you're told. Banks hate individualists, even if they say otherwise."

After the cake Bernie left to pack up his stuff. An hour later he swung by Hugo's cubicle. They promised each other once again to stay in touch. It was all very unsentimental and brief. Very masculine. The emotions were there, bubbling under surface but they both hid them as best they could. Hugo really liked Bernie. They said goodbye and then the *old timer* was gone.


Hugo spent the rest of the day trying to write but was constantly interrupted by the T-Rex who was sending him on one pointless errand after another. Paper was to be copied, reports was to be double checked, files were to be reorganized. The T-Rex was testing him.

There wasn't much he could do about it. His entire plan to write during business hours was built on the premise that the T-Rex didn't get too involved in what he was doing. If all of a sudden he started seeing Hugo as his personal assistant, he was fucked.

That afternoon he was saved by the T-Rex being called into Corporate again. The plan to merge it with Consumer was going forward and there was much to do. Around four p.m. he took a break and went over to Nella's. He noted that the people in FinCon were still working their asses off. The mood was almost hysterical. Their boss was running like a son of a bitch between cubicles trying to disarm bomb after bomb and to listen to complaints about the workload being too heavy. Everyone looked positively dead.

The contrast to Marketing was striking. They didn't seem to have anything to do at all. All the campaigns had been frozen long ago.

"That kind of thing creates tension," Hugo said.

"What?" Nella said.

"Uneven workloads."

She changed the subject. "Hugs, I think they're going to fire again."

"What have you heard?"

"When I went to the cooler to get some water I passed by Bryce's office. They were talking and the door wasn't closed all the way."

The water cooler was right outside Bryce's office. He had decided himself that it was to be placed there so that he could quench his thirst when practicing his golf swings.

"They were talking about redundancies," Nella said.

"Yeah? When will the guillotine drop?"

"They didn't say anything specific."

"It's us they're talking about, that's for sure. There's no purpose for us anymore."

"Might be time to update the CV?"

"Take it easy," Hugo tried to reassure her. "Even if it's time it might not be everyone and if anyone deserves to stay it's you."

He didn't mention the talk he had with Bernie the other day. Was Nella part of that informal group that already knew they would stay? There was no point in speculating. She couldn't tell him anyway. Not if she wanted to continue being in that group.

"I don't know if I want to stay here," she said, as if she had heard him.

"No. I get that. It'll be worse for those who'll remain."

"It won't be easy finding something else in this economy."

Hugo nodded. That was probably true. He recalled the last time he had been axed and tried to find work. It had been during the waning days of the IT-bubble and 9/11. He had sent out CV after CV without results. And things were a lot better then than they were now.

"It won't matter for you," she said. "You're going to be writer now."

He laughed. "Yeah, I'm really looking forward to being a struggling novelist. Sitting alone all day, fighting the blank page, living on canned tuna and rice, getting refused, having asshole editors fucking around with my scripts. And that's if I'm lucky! Nothing to envy."

"Why do it then?"

"I have to."

He didn't write anymore that day. When it was time to go home, Nella asked her if he wanted to come to her place.

"Have some wine. Eat something."

"No, no. I don't wanna impose. Besides, I need to sleep. I got a hot date planned with my laptop and some quality internet po'nography."

"Oh, come on! How can that really be better than spending time with moi?"

He smiled. "Not saying it is."

"Then you'll come?"

"Okay. I'll come."

He went back to his desk to collect his stuff. Just the two of them? That could be interesting.

Later when he arrived at her place he clearly noticed the sexual tension. In a way he hadn't with Nella for many years. It was way beyond that little nagging semi-attraction he had always felt for her. She made eye contact, dangled her shoe on the tip of her foot, bit her lower lip, laughed at his silly jokes, stroked her glass up and down seductively. It was on. But he held back. Restrained himself. Nella was a good friend and he didn't want take any risks. He simply excused himself early (but not so early it was rude), kissed her on the forehead and went home.

That Monday the same chainsaw consultants were back. Only this time they had a couple of high ups from New York with them. Hugo knew who they were. The global CFO and HR Head. The presence of the HR head meant personnel issues. Someone was getting sacked.

The guests wanted to use the very conference room Hugo used as his writing studio. He had to hurry back there to clean up all the printouts of the novel he had carelessly left on the big table so that they could set up their laptops there. There was no time. He quickly hid everything in the bottom drawer of a cabinet full of old office supplies, hoping that no one would develop a sudden need for a vintage 80s stapler.

"What do you think?" Nella said after he finished hooking them all up.

"Who knows, but it doesn't look like good news."

"Maybe management are the ones getting fired?"

"One can always hope."

"Maybe you'll finally get rid of Frank?"

"I don't think so," he said. "He's middle management. Or upper middle management or whatever. The top dogs won't fly in for him."

That afternoon they were all called to another meeting in the auditorium in the main lobby again. The room gave off a ghostly echo now that more than half the staff had been fired.

Management were all collected on stage again. Their navy blue suits had lost some of their sheen now and the smirky smiles were gone. Hugo and Nella sat in the back as usual. Hugo thought of Bernie. He would've been sitting in the row behind them, cracking wise, watching like the father figure with questionable morals that he was. Hugo missed him. Nella must've felt his gloomy mood. She took his hand and Hugo let it happen. They held hands for the rest of the meeting.

251

Then the CFO from New York began talking. His name was Dieter. He was German and had a thick accent. He didn't waste time and went right to it. Bryce was *moving on to new challenges*. Hardly a surprise under the circumstances. The speech had the quality of a celebration rather than that of a sacking, which was what it really was.

"Then finally he gets what he deserves," Nella said.

"Don't crack open the champagne yet," Hugo said. "He'll get so much money to leave he'll be wiping his ass with fifties for years to come."

Bryce stepped up to the mike and gave a short speech. He said something about facing the future head on and that FastCredit had to be bold and face the challenges. Hugo wasn't really listening.

"Blah, blah," he said quietly.

After the speech Bryce went around the room thanking people. He never thanked Hugo. Then he was gone. He was replaced by another guy from New York, a temporary replacement, it was said, until a permanent solution could be found.

Hugo wondered what such a permanent solution would entail. Shutting it all down?

Two weeks later news that Bryce had landed a new job reached Hugo. He was hired as a CEO at another niche bank. Same job, probably even more money and the chute from FastCredit as a bonus.

"It's not fair," Nella said when Hugo told her the news.

"No, it's not."

"Bryce should be condemned to a lifetime of unemployment after what he did here," said Benzo, who was finally back after a long time of pharmaceutical induced haze. "How is it even possible that he can do that?"

"*The Jacket Trick,*" Hugo said.

Nella smiled. "Someone should write a book about it."

Hugo smiled back.

**21**

After lunch that following Monday Nella came to his cubicle almost crying, gripping a bunch of papers so hard her knuckles were turning white. A quick glance revealed they had to do with the dangerous account transfers. He remembered she had said she had trouble with it. It was worse than he had thought.

"I'll help you," Hugo said. "But first we need to cool it. We'll go to the kitchen and get a cup of coffee. Then you'll go get all the material you have and a laptop. Then we'll go to one of the conference rooms and have a look."

She calmed down and they went to get the coffee. It doesn't matter what has happened. There's always a legitimate reason to get another cup of coffee before addressing anything.

"It'll be okay," he said. He hoped he was right. Budgeting wasn't exactly his strong suit. It had never been his job but four eyes are usually better than two.

Nella started elaborating already on the way to the conference room. Hugo quieted her down.

"Careful. Everyone here has shotgun mikes for ears.

Don't wanna give the cheese more ammo than they already have."

Well inside, she started again. She had found the error she had been talking about. There was money missing. A lot of it.

"I transferred too much money. I forgot some of the defaulted loans. I should've double checked everything. The procedure clearly says you have to double check and maybe I didn't?"

"What you're saying is that management have spent money they didn't really have?"

"Exactly. Since I missed transferring those defaulted loans it looked like there was more than there really was."

"Is it fixable?"

"No. The money is gone."

It wasn't her fault. Anyone could've made that mistake. Especially these last few months.

"All I can do is confess I made a mistake," she said. "And hope they don't fire me. Or worse, press charges or something."

"No, no. Relax. They won't press charges, silly."

"Maybe not. But this hurts me. Stuff like this goes on your permanent record."

She was right about that. Anyone can make mistakes but when you cost the bank money it's never good. This time it was a lot of money. A couple of hundred thousand at least. Nella could expect a good spanking. A metaphorical one, of course.

"Okay," Hugo said. "Let me think for an hour or so. I'll fix it. I promise."

"Okay."

"When's it due?"

"Tomorrow."

He followed Nella back to her place. He gave her a hug. He kissed her cheek. She was calmer now. If only a little.

On his way back to his cubicle he ran into the T-Rex. He was strolling around the landscape, nose in the air, as if he was trying to see over the cubicle walls.

*He's checking to see if I'm in at my desk.*

When the T-Rex saw him he charged.

"What's your excuse this time?" the T-Rex asked.

Hugo gave him a deliberately confused look, then a sigh.

"What do you mean?" he said.

"No attitude, please. Just answer the question."

Despite everything that had happened over the last few months, Hugo's new slacker attitude towards working, his decision to write a novel and not get frustrated with the T-Rex, he couldn't help but get angry. It was a reflex, deeply sown into his spinal cord. He forced himself to cool off. He wasn't going to get into a big fight here, out in the open.

"I was in FinCon," he said. "I was helping Nella with something. She had a few questions about our portfolio with bad loans. I hope it's okay to help co-workers who ask for it?"

The T-Rex gave him the stink eye. Like one of those exaggerated, comical ones Tom makes when Jerry steals his milk. He didn't believe him. Ironically, since for once he was actually telling the truth.

"Okay," the T-Rex finally said. He was starting to get red again. He turned abruptly and left, kind of like a child after being told he's grounded for the weekend.

Hugo stopped by the kitchen before returning to his desk. He grabbed the biggest cup he could find and filled it with black coffee. He topped it off with an espresso and a dash of milk. A coke from the freezer would complete his caffeine bomb. He needed the extra boost if he was to help Nella.

The caffeine proved unnecessary. He was finished before he even sat down. There was really only one way to solve the problem. He knew what he had to do. He went back to her.

"We'll say I did it," he said.

Nella shook her head. "No. Absolutely not!"

"Think about it. I'm fucked here anyway. It's just a question of time before I'm caught. The T-Rex is on my ass like a bad case of hemorrhoids. Management already hates my guts. I have nothing to lose. You have everything to lose."

"You do have something to lose! What about your severance package? If they fire you you'll be making sandwiches at Subway. You can kiss the writing goodbye."

"Screw it! We'll go to your boss and tell him together. We'll say I helped you and I screwed up. I'll take the heat."

"But it's wrong." She looked down at the floor and didn't say anything else.

"Okay?" Hugo said again.

"Okay. They can't see who really did the transfer then?"

"No. Since it's done with a spreadsheet it can't be traced. Relax. It'll work."

Gary... *something*, was the name of Nella's boss. Hugo didn't know much about him except that he had been at FastCredit for about a year. When the T-Rex stripped Hugo of all work he had lost all contact with the top level and because of that he had never really gotten to know him.

They both went into his office that afternoon and explained. Hugo didn't know exactly what to expect from Gary. Was he smart? Would he see through the lie? Hugo had managed to convince him earlier to let Nells go to Paris with him so there was a precedent.

His concerns proved to be unfounded. Gary-*something* bought it all. Hugo added that he was the one who had constructed the spreadsheet once upon a time. That the sheet's inherent fallacies were his doing. In truth, it had come as is from New York years ago, before Hugo even worked at FastCredit. Nobody at the top would know such a detail. That little cherry would make Hugo doubly accountable and shift even more suspicion away from Nella.

"I have to take this up with the rest of the management team," Gary said. "You understand?"

"Do what you have to do," Hugo said. "I'll take responsibility for my goof."

"I'll do my best to keep you out of the discussion but it'll be hard. They'll want a name."

Hugo nodded. Management would probably launch a full investigation. The T-Rex would find out. It would probably give him what he needed to get Hugo fired.

The day after he was called into the T-Rex's office. Just as Hugo thought, they were launching an inquiry. Since it was a manual work-around Hugo would be shown some leniency. He could hardly take the blame for the lack of adequate controls in their computer systems.

"But between you and me," the T-Rex said, smiling, "it doesn't look good for you. I'm going to recommend a course of action with regards to your continued employment here based on this inquiry. And you haven't exactly convinced me that you're a valuable resource for us. I'd advise you to start packing now. If management follows my recommendations you are finished."

Straight shooter. The T-Rex had made up his mind. No surprise there.

When Hugo left he was both angry and relieved. It would mean that the T-Rex would win the game but at the same time he was kind of glad it would all be over soon. But mostly he was happy for Nella. For whatever reason she liked it here, despite her occasional light whining, and he had managed to keep her out of it.

Later that evening he lay in bed and thought about today's events.

*The hero is in dire straits.*

This was perfect for the book. He liked playing the part of the self-sacrificing hero who rescues the damsel in distress. But the thought hit him that it was a just little too convenient. This turn of events was just what the story needed and now it just appeared out of nowhere. Again he started having those strange doubts about himself. Did it happen or was he imagining it?

*Of course it happened!*

Didn't it? Sure, people make mistakes. That happens all the time so Nella's part was certainly true. But people don't step in and take the fall for others like he had just done. People aren't wired like that. Certainly not him. People are selfish and rational.

*Just look what I did to Jess. If I was the self-sacrificing type I would've stayed with her.*

People protect themselves and avoid accountability whenever they can. Hugo had never claimed to be any different. So why did he take the fall for Nella? It didn't make sense. Was he in love with her? He liked her and was kind of hot for her, but love? He didn't think so.

*Unless I didn't do it at all. I made it up in my head. Fuck, have I gone off the deep end?*

The room was spinning now. He felt nauseous. He closed his eyes, forced himself to think of something else. He thought about work. Actual real work. Shuffling papers and moving decimals. Nothing grounds you like a little boring office work. It worked. The strange feeling slowly gave way to boredom. And then to sleepiness. He dozed off, and for the rest of the night he was in a virtual coma. The next day he had forgotten about it all.


The days passed by. Nothing much happened. The T-Rex was again back at Corporate and Hugo could write in relative peace. Three quarters of the book was now on paper and he was beginning to get a feel for the finished result. The fact that he had so much peace and quiet worried him. It could only mean the T-Rex had everything he needed to win the game.

That Wednesday they were all gathered again at *The Tick*. Even Benzo were there. He was currently seeing a shrink and had one of his better periods now.

Nella was buying, as a thanks to Hugo for taking the rap for her. Maia was working the bar but Lardy still couldn't join them. Some delivery had gone wrong and that kept him in the office in the back, making phone calls to clear the whole thing up. But Maia was becoming quite adept at swinging bottles around days.

"*Tom-Cruise*-in-*Cocktail* style!" Nicolas said.

"Uh-oh. Lame Eighties reference alert!" Nella said.

"Fuck you."

Benzo didn't much care about the fact that drinking while having his kind of problems wasn't such a great idea. He quickly got pretty sped up. He retold Hugo's heroics enthusiastically. Hugo now regretted ever telling him about it.

"Damn," Nicolas said. "My hero!"

"*My* hero," Nella said. "But I feel for Hugo. Now he'll be in trouble." She caressed his arm.

Benzo continued his tale by telling them about the inquiry and how the T-Rex practically had promised to fire him.

"So, what's the plan?" Nicolas said. "Any more aces up your sleeve?"

"Not really. I don't know what to do. If the T-Rex has decided, I guess I'm cooked."

"So you're just going to let him win?"

"I'll just keep going until something happens. I'll write as much as I can and collect as many paychecks as I can. Besides, I might still make it. Management can still choose not to go with ol' Rexie."

"How much influence does that geezer really have?" Nicolas asked.

"I honestly don't know. Officially he's just middle

management, but he managed to weasel his way in with the head cheeses. I don't know how. I thought he was their puppet but sometimes it seems like he's the puppet *master*."

Hugo took a sip of his beer.

"He still doesn't know anything about the writing?" Nicolas said.

"He suspects something is up, that I'm sure of."

"I have to say I'm impressed by what you've done. Crazy, sure, but yeah. I'm impressed. You're the only one with an ego big enough to pull something like that off. A toast!"

Hugo wasn't sure if that was a compliment or an insult. Never mind. They drank. Nella signaled to Maia to bring another round.

They were done at around midnight. Hugo didn't have anyone to hurry home to anymore and he wasn't going to be in tomorrow until his usual time around eleven, so there was really no reason to go home yet. He didn't want to.

*As soon as you're single you get urge to go to nightclubs and whatnot. The very thought of those meat markets disgust you when you're paired up. Unless you're tired of fucking her, that is. Which of course you are, so you end up going anyway. Then you sit there like an idiot at the bar gawking at all the hot girls writhing on the dance floor, none of whom you have the guts to approach.*

He kept Nella company to the bus as usual.

"Have you heard anything about the inquiry yet?"

"It'll be done this week."

He actually had a meeting scheduled with the T-Rex the following Thursday. No agenda had been appended, but Hugo knew what it was about.

"What do you think?" she asked.

"I think I'm screwed."

Nella took his arm and held it the rest of the way to the bus. They didn't speak. It wasn't necessary.

**22**

Time crawled by, but that Thursday still came eventually. The T-Rex had been away all morning and it was shortly before lunch when he showed up at Hugo's cubicle to remind him of their meeting.

At three the hammer would fall. Hugo was nervous. The jitters spread throughout his body like a virus, despite having being through many similar situations with the T-Rex by now. He hadn't prepared anything this time. No glorious defense speech, no tricks and illusions. It would just be him against the dinosaur.

To stay calm he did everything he could think of except working. Not on the novel or anything else. He ran back and forth to the kitchen to refill his coffee. He went down to the lobby but didn't sit in the sofa. He paced back and forth in the big hall. All those thoughts were driving him insane.

He ate his lunch alone. The cafeteria was big and it was rarely a problem to find a distant corner, away from everyone. When he came back up the chainsaw people were back. They sat together with the temp boss from New York, the guy that had replaced Bryce.

He went over to Nella and told her.

"So what do you think?"

"This time it has to do with us."

"It'll all be over soon," she said.

Hugo saw Benzo walking with a machine under his arm. Hugo waved him over to tell him about the chainsaw people. He didn't have to. Benzo had already seen them.

"Round two, then?" he said. "I really hope I'm going in this one. I can't fucking stand this place anymore."

"I hear you," Hugo said. "I don't think anyone else can either."

"And you? Your meeting with the Rex?"

Hugo nodded. "At three."

"Nervous?"

"Yes."

"Let me know if I can do anything. Maybe wreck his account so that he can't access any of his applications? Or maybe I can find some dirt on his drive? Some kiddy porn or him in drag or whatever. Threaten to send it to Layla!"

Hugo laughed.

"Thanks, but I'll fight my own battles."

"As any true hero does," Benzo said and smiled. "Good luck. I have to go beat the crap out this machine." He motioned to the machine under his arm. "Layla spilled coffee on this one. Again."

After talking to Benzo and Nella, Hugo tried to actually get some writing done but the blank page was too powerful today. Instead he whipped up a latte in the kitchen and went for a stroll in the park down by the Thames. He stared at his watch. Sometimes he was sure the batteries had died. The dials just wouldn't move. It was all like watching cement dry. But no matter how slowly it seems time passes, it does. It was finally time.

The T-Rex closed the door behind them and closed the blinds two thirds of the way. They still let in some light from the hallway outside but you wouldn't be able to see in or out. The T-Rex apparently wanted to make this as private as he could. If he wanted Hugo to feel trapped and claustrophobic, he had succeeded.

*Don't talk first. Don't give the old prick the satisfaction.*

The T-Rex rubbed his palms against each other as usual. Hugo could feel a droplet of sweat forming in the hairline above his forehead. It would soon start sliding down, over his temple and onto his cheek.

*Really! Sweating? I'm such a cliché.*

Not very hero-like at all. Finally the T-Rex spoke.

"Okay, Hugo."

Then he went back to rubbing his palms. Then he pretended (Hugo at least thought it looked fake) to go through some papers on the desk.

"The inquiry..."

Went through some more papers.

"The inquiry..."

Rubbed palms.

"*The inquiry*....came to the conclusion that it was negligent of you not to double check the transfers as per protocol."

So far no surprises.

The T-Rex really seemed to enjoy this. Since he started talking he had had a distinct smirk on his lips, in his eyes a sadistic look. Hugo made an additional effort not to seem affected by the theatrics. Show no worry. No doubt.

"Management found it enough to give you a warning," the T-Rex said. "An official warning that goes on your permanent record. You'll get it in writing."

Hugo exhaled, but T-Rex still smirking. If anything, even more now. Hugo didn't understand why. The T-Rex had lost. Management only gave him a warning. What gives?

The T-Rex rubbed his palms. Then he grabbed a new bunch of papers from his desk drawer. Hugo immediately saw that it was prints from his novel. He swallowed hard and completely lost his poker face.

*Where the fuck did he get those? Fuck! The drawer in the conference room.*

He never cleaned it out after the chainsaw people had left. He knew he shouldn't have printed anything at work. But he couldn't edit on screen. He needed paper. To write notes in the margins. To underline important passages and so forth. He thought he had been careful but obviously not careful enough.

"You know what this is," the T-Rex said. It was a statement, not a question.

Hugo didn't say anything.

"You don't have to speak. I know you wrote this."

It was all over. The book revealed everything. All the tricks. That he had been writing during company time. That he had scammed the T-Rex and everyone else here. All of it! He couldn't quite see what part of the novel the T-Rex had gotten his hands on but it wouldn't matter. He was FUCKED!

*No, I'm not just fucked. I'm royally fucked. I'm more fucked than a hooker in a Soho walk-up.*

The T-Rex cheeks were all red again. He slammed the pages hard against the desk. He was furious, of course. Who wouldn't have been if they found out they'd been scammed like this? It was humiliating, ridiculing. Hugo still wasn't going to give in without a proper fight.

"You can't prove anything," he said. "I could've made all that up. After all the story is pretty outrageous. Who will believe that anyone actually has the balls to do something like that? Who will believe that someone is stupid enough to fall for it like you did? The way I spun tales around you? Played you like you were a retarded puppet. Huh?"

*Yeah, who would?*

That funny dizzy feeling came back. He felt a bit nauseous and the room was beginning to spin. Not much, but still. He didn't have time to wallow in self-doubt right now. He focused on the T-Rex. His face, his reddening cheeks. The pressure cooker was about to blow again. It worked. The nausea was subsiding, the spinning stopped. The T-Rex stood up, his chair exploded backwards and hit the wall hard.

"DO YOU THINK I'M AN IDIOT?"

"Well duh! I said just that, didn't I?"

"You'll pay for this! Trust me. I WILL take this to the management team."

His breathing was heavy and his cheeks were almost

purple.

"You have defrauded the bank! You've lifted paychecks here but haven't worked for them. It's fraud. FRAUD!"

Hugo watched how a fat strand of saliva tore itself lose from the side of the T-Rex's moth when he yelled 'FRAUD'. It seemed to go in slow motion. The larger part of the glob landed on Hugo's manuscript. It splattered across the pages. A small strand hit Hugo's forehead. He was in such shock he didn't even wipe it off. The T-Rex slammed the papers again. More saliva splattered. It was nasty. He much preferred Katja's brand of face-splattering, gross as it had been.

"I'll talk to the management team on Monday. They're busy today and tomorrow with the consultants. I will recommend you be terminated. You should be glad if we don't press charges."

Hugo didn't say anything else. There was no point. Nella and Benzo met him immediately after he came out of the T-Rex's office. He wiped his face clean of the spit.

"So?" Benzo said.

Hugo told them.

"So, a warning for the transfer thing, but you go anyway."

Nella seemed relieved. Hugo understood. She didn't bear any more responsibility for him being fired. That the T-Rex had caught him was nobody's fault but his own.

"So what's the plan?" Nella asked.

"I'm going to have to break out the big guns," he said. "The fucker spat in my face. Not intentionally. It was anger spit. But still."

"So what's the big guns," Benzo said.

"I have until Monday. That's when he'll speak to the cheese. Plenty of time for my final move."

"Which is?"

"I'm going to have sex with Layla."


He had it all planned out. Rex was out of office today so Layla would definitely drive home alone. It wouldn't have mattered. She usually left before Rex and they always drove separate cars.

He would wait by her car. Chat her up. Go home with her. Give her a couple of, hopefully, earth shattering orgasms, get the hell out before the T-Rex got home. Rex was at the corporate branch today so that meant he would be home late. Otherwise maybe he could persuade her to go to his place. But that was definitely plan B. He wanted to go to their place. He wanted to fuck her on Rex's home turf, in their marital bed.

*It would be soooo sweeet!!!*

"Well, well. Hugo," she said when she saw him. "Fancy seeing you here."

"Actually it's Hugs. My friends call me Hugs."

"Hugs. Cute. What are you doing here? Looking for an excuse to see me?"

She smiled and Hugo couldn't quite tell if she was joking or not. He went with it.

"You caught me. I can't get that almost fuck out of my mind. You stirred something up and now you're paying the price."

"Oh, really?"

The cocky-funny banter went on for a while. He had

a whole evening planned with clever incremental steps to get her more and more into it in case her interest had cooled a bit. Increased touching, gradual eye contact intensification, the works. He was just about to suggest coffee, to start things off. Such groundwork proved unnecessary.

"You know Frank won't be home until late," she said and bit her lower lip.

"Oh, you're naughty. Naughty. Naughty girl."

"I can be, if I like to."

He took two steps closer, now standing just inches away from her. He could smell her perfume, her breath, with just a hint of office coffee and cigarettes.

"Are you suggesting what I think you're suggesting?"

She didn't say anything. She just stood there looking fuck all sexy and seductive. He went for the kiss. A full blown kiss this time.

"Let's go," she said.

They got in the car and she drove them to hers and the T-Rex's place. They played touchy as much as it was possible with her driving. He caressed her leg, she went for his crotch. He was hard by the time they were there.

They continued the foreplay into the apartment, tearing off items of clothing along the way. She pulled him into bed with him on top of her. He looked her in the eyes. They were beautiful. There wasn't just lust in there. There was something else. Sadness. He hesitated.

*Not like this.*

It would've been a spectacular way to get back at the T-Rex by fucking his wife, but he couldn't do it. A real hero wouldn't do such a thing. He couldn't resolve the plot that way! Adultery as revenge. What a massive, tired old cliché.

"I'm sorry," he said. "I can't."

She was confused at first. But she understood. It wasn't a rejection. He could see that she knew it was wrong too. They ended up talking for a few hours instead.

"I know you just wanted to fuck me to get back at Frank," she said. "I know all about the problems he has with you. Or that you have with him."

"Is that why you're so attracted to me?"

"Maybe. Do you care?"

"No. Question is, what is *your* beef with the man? Why did *you* almost fuck *me*?"

"Don't get me started. I've had it with that infertile wimp. We haven't had anything physical for years."

"Really? Infertile?"

"We're in our fifties. Do you see any pictures of kids here?"

He didn't.

"He doesn't allow me to have pictures of my kids from my previous marriage at home. That's why I keep everything in my office."

"So it's true. He really doesn't allow you to have pictures of your own kids in your house? That's so sad."

She nodded. "Yes, it's true. He still loves me. I'm sure of that."

"Sorry to hear that. But hey, it probably hurts him to see pictures of kids, knowing he can't give you any. Still, it's definitely douchy."

She looked sad again, maybe a little guilty, but didn't say anything. Hugo thought it was best not to pry any deeper into this.

The age-old story. People fear loneliness more than they fear a loveless relationship. It's better to grind sexes once every three months to keep up the statistics and fool yourself you're living a passionate and exciting life than admit that you're dry inside.

He got dressed, kissed her on the forehead and left.


That Friday the T-Rex would finally have his meeting with the temp boss from New York and the rest of the management team. It was to take place in one hour.

*One hour.*

That was how long he had left as an employee at FastCredit. He would be asked to clean out his desk immediately after the meeting was done.

He met the T-Rex in the kitchen.

"I hope you know this is nothing personal," he said while stirring his coffee. He held out a hand for Hugo to shake.

"Really? After all this, you're going with the 'it's nothing personal'-speech?"

"Very well," the T-Rex said and went back to his office.

Benzo and Nella joined him, gave him reassuring pats on the back, telling him it wasn't all that bad to get fired and so forth. Nothing new, really. Hugo only mourned for his lost severance. They wouldn't give him shit after what he'd done.

They spent that hour down in the sofa in the main lobby. Just talking. Like old times. The hour passed, not as slowly as he would have thought. Maybe because he wasn't nervous this time. He was beyond such petty emotions now.

They were just about go back up again when two uniformed police officers showed up at the front desk. After being cleared by the receptionist they headed for FastCredit's offices. Hugo, Benzo and Nella just stared at each other.

"What the...?" Benzo said.

They followed them back up, making sure to keep a respectable distance. FastCredit's receptionist led the police to the room where the management team were having their meeting. A few minutes later they came out with the T-Rex in cuffs. He was all red faced. He averted his gaze, keeping his eyes pointed towards the ground. He was clearly ashamed as the police took him away. The whole staff had stopped working now and were looking, jaws dropped.

"Who said *deus ex machina* is an outdated plot device?" Hugo said. The others looked at him, confused. Benzo gave him a pat on the shoulder. Hugo looked at him, thinking about what Benzo had said earlier about breaking into the T-Rex's personal drive.

"What?" Benzo said.

"Benzo?"

"What!"

Hugo just smiled.

They all just went back to their desks without saying anything else. Hugo did what he had done the last few months. He wrote.

It turned out that the T-Rex had burned down his own summer home for the insurance money. Rumors were running wild. One said that he owed the mob money.    Another suggested that he had murdered someone and kept the body in the basement and that he had burned down the house to destroy the evidence. And that wasn't even the worst one. They would never know exactly what happened.  Hugo never heard anything about the book from the rest of the management. He never heard from the T-Rex again.

**23**

*Sometime later....*

The office. The Purgatory of real life. On the other side awaited the sweet release of death, but he had no way of getting there.

*Didn't I put something like that in the book?*

The book. He hadn't written anything in a few months now ever since the showdown. He had gone back to shuffling papers and moving decimals in his spreadsheets. For real. No tricks this time. No lies. No jacket hanging over the back of his chair. Ever since the T-Rex left he had hit the wall. Writer's block. He had been left alive after the climax but there was no victory in the fall out. Just this. The never ending tedium of office work.

He never realized he actually needed the T-Rex that much. Ol' Rexie had been the bow that accelerated the arrow towards its target but now there was no tension in the string. No adrenaline rushes. No coal to fuel the creative furnace. No need to keep mocking him by writing that damned book instead of working.

He finished another sheet while the web radio he had brought in for his tricks kept playing non-offensive pop hits in the background (but he turned it off now when he left).

The police coming to get T-Rex was sort of a letdown. Sure, he achieved his goal of not getting fired. His new boss was another clueless tool (they all are). He never checked in on Hugo, never insisted on updates or any kind of control of his whereabouts. The crisis had deepened so much now that nobody checked up on anybody anymore. Nobody gave a shit and everyone was firmly snuggled up in the job protection phase. FastCredit finally, was a rooster that kept running around despite having been decapitated long ago. Technically Hugs could do what he wanted, but it wasn't the same.

Every once in a while he brought up the book and read a few paragraphs. He truly didn't know what to do with the ending. The T-Rex was gone, but his hero never got to defeat him on his own terms. The cops just came and swept him away from under him. You can't end a story like that! It's cheating. Everybody know the cops are supposed to show up *after* the hero disposed of the bad guy by himself.

Nella had lost interest in him as well. It felt that way, at least. He knew it was because he never defeated his nemesis. What love interest can have the hots for a leading man who gets rescued by the police? It's lame and no woman would ever fall in love with someone who doesn't win his own fights. It's what Hollywood teaches us and it turns out to be true.

There was no trace of their earlier interactions. They met in the kitchen, got their coffee, talked work, no eye contact, no innocent touching of shoulders or smalls of backs. No heat whatsoever. It was like it all never happened. The talks in the sofa downstairs, the park and the mutual understanding around voluntary childlessness were all gone.

*Maybe it actually never did happen?*

Layla was gone too. She dumped the Rex and quit her job. Nobody had heard from her since.

*Maybe Nella was right. He really couldn't tell the difference between his book and reality anymore? Some pretty awesome things did happen. The tricks. The fire alarms. Him almost fucking Layla. Twice! Katja and getting spat in the face with his own cum!*

*I mean, come on! How often do things like that really happen? Life's long and boring, remember!*

Jess was gone too. She had picked up the last of her stuff a month ago. Hugo barely made rent anymore with only one income. He was at least pretty sure his relationship with her had been real. Both metaphysically and emotionally. He remembered the scene where she had accused him of seeing their relationship as a joke. At the restaurant where she had thrown her glass of wine in his face.

*What the fuck! Who does something so cruel?*

He meant himself, of course. Taking it all as a joke and going on about the book. He deserved that wine in the face.

It was all a lie. The tricks, the fucking, the T-Rex, Nella. Maybe even Bernie. Like the Jacket Trick itself, they had all been illusions. After all, none of them were here anymore. Well, Nella was, but not the Nella he knew. Or thought he knew. All that was left was a boring, depressing office with boring gray office people. Including himself. That was what was definitely real.

*It couldn't be all be fake? Could it?*

He had to find out. These thoughts had been eating at him for weeks now. The itch was becoming progressively worse and he just had to scratch it. Right now. It was too much. He looked frantically around his cubicle for anything, *anything* that could prove to him that the stuff in the book was real.

*Anything. For the love of God!*

*Did I just make a reference to God! Shit, now I know I'm losing it.*

He peeked outside his cubicle. No T-Rex. No Bryce. No Bernie. No Nella shooting him glances of affection or anger because he berated banking or management. Not even Benzo was still here. He had gone off to some rehab facility in Germany for benzo abusers.

*I'm fucking losing it! Driven insane by office work.*

He looked around but found nothing that could help him.

*The radio!*

The radio was playing. He did bring that in for a trick, didn't he? He could hear it, playing Sade, or Allison Moyet, or something similarly lame from the Eighties. It was real. Definitely. Those tunes were as boring and pointless as the office.

He knew what he had to do now. He had to prove to himself that this was real. That this place was real. That the crazy shit he had done was real. No more lies. No Jacket Tricks. Just the naked truth.

*Naked! The rebirth! It's time to be reborn, finally.*

He had to get up and just leave. Quit the job. Walk out of here with nothing. Leave it all behind except the naked truth. Just like when you're born. He had to go, naked, into a new world. A world where he was a writer, not some dude working in a bank. He had to shoot out of the confining womb that was this place. To cut the umbilical cord. This office. Money. Security. He didn't need it.

*The book!*

He had to save the book. He managed to open up an e-mail, attach the manuscript and send it off to his private address. Safe. If the book was real, if writing it like he did was indeed real, he sure as hell wasn't going to waste it.

He moved his desk out from the wall into the center of his cubicle, got up on it and kicked the walls around him. He kicked them hard several time until they all fell. People turned to see what all the thumping was all about. The walls made a loud smack when they hit the floor. The whole office could see him now and he could see them.

"To be reborn," he said to himself.

He started stripping off his clothes. All the way down. He felt the breeze from the air conditioner on his junk. He noticed he hadn't trimmed in a while. He looked around, saw how his colleagues reacted to his nude, pale body. Some were horrified, some of the girls giggled. The guys laughed and applauded.

"Wuuuuuu-huuuuuu!"

Hugo just smiled. This felt real. At last something that felt real. He gave them all the finger, both hands.

He danced around a little.

He grabbed his junk. "Fuck you all! I'm quitting."

He jumped down from the table and started walking. More people were applauding, whistling. Others were hiding their faces in their hands, blushing with embarrassment. Some were screaming things.

"Way to go, Hugs! Nice package! Cold in here, huh? Wu-huuuu!"

No one tried to stop him.

They formed a corridor around him as he headed confidently towards the exit, his hairy cock and balls dangling back and forth, making smacking sounds against his thighs as he strode. He blew kisses to the girls along the way. When he reached the front door one of the girls used her access card to open it for him. She was laughing hysterically.

Some followed him through the lobby to the reception. Hugs just kept going.

When he was at the big rotating doors he turned around. There she was. Nella, her hand covering her mouth, her eyes wet with tears, but happy.

"See you, Hugs?" she said.

He smiled. "See you, Nella." He winked at her, flirtatiously, in the lame kind of way. It just seemed appropriate for this moment.

He turned around and went through the doors and out in the streets. After a while he noticed nobody was following him anymore. New people, in outdoor clothing were looking strangely at him now. Detached interest. A naked guy. Big deal.

Now he was finally reborn. His banking career was dead. No more office. No more paper pushing. No more need for the jacket trick.  He decided that's what he was going to call the book.  *The Jacket Trick.*

Now it had its fucking ending!

*The hero rides off into the sunset.  Turn the last page and on to the afterword!  The author would like to thank....blah, blah, blah.  Ah, screw it.  Nobody reads those anyway.*

## ACKNOWLEDGEMENTS

The author would like to acknowledge the following people for providing crucial insight for this book in terms of criticism and editing. Richard Blandford, Victoria Budkevich, Dorota Gorna, Julia Gibbs, Kaare Hansson and Margareth Hansson.

André Hansson
March 2014

For more content visit:

www.thejackettrick.com

Printed in Great Britain
by Amazon